HOLDING OUT

BALLARAT CHARTER

LILA ROSE

Hawks MC: Ballarat Charter: Book 1

Editing: Hot Tree Editing

Interior Design: Rogena Mitchell-Jones

Fourth Edition 2019

ISBN: 978-0648481607

CHAPTER ONE

With a bloody nose and legs, a split lip and wild tremor going through my body, I picked up the phone and called the one person I knew would help me."Hey, wench, you never call from the house phone… what's wrong?" My best friend's voice had started out happy, then suddenly taken on the edge of panic.

"I-I, Dee, I need your help," I whispered and looked over my shoulder to my passed-out husband on the bed.

On the bed where he had just beaten and raped me.

Yes, we were married; still, no meant no. Cries of pain meant something was wrong. Screaming meant that the one who caused it should stop.

But he didn't.

My husband invaded my body and mind, ruining me

in so many ways. I wanted him to pay for what he did. I wanted him to hurt.

But I was scared, and I only saw one way out of it all.

To run.

"I'm coming, Zara," Deanna uttered into the phone and then hung up.

Knowing my husband was so high and drunk that he wouldn't wake, even if the house exploded around him, I started to pack.

Deanna must have heard the urgency in my voice; the journey that would usually take half an hour only took her fifteen minutes. My husband knew nothing of Deanna, and I was glad I'd kept it that way. He hated me having friends; he hated me doing a lot of things, and stupidly I had listened to him at the start. Because back then he was different, he showed me the world and told me that he and I were going to shine through it all.

It took him a year to change, to become his true self, a man I would never have married if I had known how cruel he was. He liked things his way or no way at all.

Deanna came running into the bedroom; I had given her a key months ago, worried something like this would happen. She looked from me to the bed.

"That motherfucker." Her hand went behind her and when she pulled it back around it held a gun.

"No," I cried, my hand going around her wrist as she pointed it at David.

Deanna turned her hard gaze to me. "Look at what he did to you, hun. He—"

"Please, Dee. Please understand I don't want his death on my conscience. He will be more hurt and pissed if we let him be and he wakes finding me gone. I need to get out of here, honey. I need to find a place where he can't find me."

"I want to hurt him, Zara. I want to gut the fucking pig." Tears filled her eyes as she noticed the blood running down my thighs from under my short nightie.

A sob tore through me. "I want to make him pay in the worst way…and me leaving, escaping him when he thought I couldn't and wouldn't, will be my revenge. Please, please, hun."

"Jesus," she snapped, shaking off my hold on her arm and reaching for my cases. "Are you okay to walk?"

"Y-yes." I sent her a pathetic smile and started for the door.

I wouldn't look back. David was now a part of my past, and he deserved nothing from me from that day on. No thought, no tears…nothing.

Deanna was my guiding light. She had been since I met her at the library in our book group. From that night on she was more so. She took me from that house to hers; there she helped me clean up and after we started to make plans.

From her computer I emailed my parents, telling

them I was now out from under David's thumb, but I needed time to make sure things would be safe for all of us. I couldn't and wouldn't risk my parents' or brother's lives going back to them. So I moved, with Deanna, to another state. It was there I found out David had left me with last parting gift…I was pregnant. And I would say gift, because when Maya was born my heart couldn't think of her as anything but special. She was my new world and I would do anything to keep her safe.

SIX YEARS LATER

I was enjoying the walk home in the afternoon sun. My boss had an assignment and she kindly gave me the rest of the day off. Maya, my six-year-old, was attending the school sleepover for her grade. So I picked myself up some chocolate, a DVD, a bottle of wine, and Chinese takeout for dinner. Even better, my best friend, Deanna was coming over later to help me make the most of my relaxing night in.

I rounded the corner to my street and froze. My annoying, but hot neighbour was standing out the front of my other neighbour's house talking to the Campbells' nineteen-year-old daughter, Karen. I hung my head, ready to stride past, humming a tune along the way to cover their voices. Still, her high cackle broke through, as irritating as always. I was close to freedom and just past them, deafening myself with my out-of-tune hum when someone grabbed my arm and spun me back around.

"Kitten," Talon said.

My eyes closed of their own accord to cherish the sound. It happened every time I heard his deep grumble of a voice.

"Uh, what? Oh, Talon?" I blushed and bit my bottom lip.

He laughed. "I asked where Maya was."

"Oh, um, she's at school. Her class is having a sleep-over," I informed him. Though I didn't know why.

"Right. So…." he began but stopped to look into my shopping bags. "We're watching *27 Dresses,* eating Chinese, and drinking wine. Sounds like a plan. What time do you want me to come over? I could bring dessert." He grinned mischievously.

I looked around him to Karen. She huffed something and stomped off. I then turned my gaze back to the hunk with his messy, needs-a-cut black hair and dark brown eyes.

I'd never forgotten the day I moved onto the street and into my three-bedroom weatherboard home two years ago and learned that I was living across the road from the local biker compound, with their head honcho right next door to me. I had just moved with Maya out of Deanna's house after being there for four years. I was feeling frightened and overwhelmed, as well as a little inebriated after having a few welcome-to-the-new-house drinks with Deanna. Deanna left and I was in bed, but Maya kept waking up from the loud music being played next door. After she drifted back to sleep for the third time, I went—armed with the confidence of the alcohol—next door, dressed in my pink nightie with a kitten on the front and combat boots. I banged on the door. A short, hairy guy opened it and raised his eyebrows at me.

"Who is the freaking owner of this place?" I demanded.

"Yo, boss," the man called over his shoulder.

And I swear my heart stopped when Talon walked his broad, muscular form my way dressed in jeans and a white tee with a leather vest hanging open over it. Everything but him faded into the background.

"Whadup, cupcake?" He leaned against the doorframe and crossed his arms over his chest.

My eyes closed. Until I remembered, I was there for a reason, and that reason was more important than Mr Hotness.

Upon opening them, I went straight into a glare that could scare most young children. His mouth twitched. "I just moved in next door. I thought 'wow, what a nice place to start anew! That was until your bloody stupid music started blasting on a freakin' Monday night. I have a daughter who is starting her new school tomorrow." I stepped up closer. "Turn down the music. *Now*," I hissed.

"Wow, boss, you have a fuckin' wildcat living next door," someone said from behind him. Manly chuckles began. I ignored the others and kept my glare on bossman.

"More like a wild kitten." He smiled, looking down at my nightie. "Don't worry, kitten. I'll turn down the music. But, it'll cost you."

I blanched and stepped back, all confidence gone. "Wh...what?"

The men laughed louder.

"Just one kiss, babe."

"Talon!" A woman growled from somewhere behind the laughing crowd.

"You're a... pig," I said and walked away. Not long after that, the music was turned down.

From that day on, no matter how many times I tried to dodge Talon Marcus, I still managed to bump into him and make a fool of myself—something that he greatly enjoyed. I could tell from his small teasing smirks or laughter at my expense because he knew what he did to me and my libido. He enjoyed playing games with me... and okay, sometimes I even enjoyed them, deep, deep down. Because every time something happened, he made me feel desired.

However, feeling *that* scared me, and in turn, caused me to become a chicken, so to avoid the man who invaded my dreams I spent a lot of time with my daughter at Deanna's.

An example of why I had to steer clear of such hotness was what happened four days ago. Maya was at Deanna's while I quickly ran home to do a few errands and clean the house without my daughter making more of a mess. I had just gotten out of my car when Talon magically appeared out of nowhere.

"Kitten." He smiled.

Upon opening my eyes, I squeaked, "Talon," and tried to walk around him. He wouldn't have it of course and stepped in front of me.

"What are you doin' tonight?" he asked, and I watched as his hands slowly rose to tuck my long wavy hair behind my shoulder. My eyes stayed glued to his hand as his fingers gently ran down my arm to my hand. There his fingers wrapped around mine and tugged.

"Kitten," he chuckled.

Shaking my head, I looked up and glared at the bad, bad biker man.

God, he loved playing with me.

Still, even though my body loved to be played with, I was no longer that woman.

The woman who risked.

And it was a guess, but I was sure it was a good guess that Talon Marcus, president of the Hawks Motorcycle Club, was one huge risk to my heart.

"I'm,"—I licked my dry lips, my eyes widening when his beautiful eyes watched my tongue—"I'm busy, um, it was, ah, really nice to see you, Talon, but I have to go," I blurted, and then to my… disgrace, practically ran to my front door with his deep chuckle following me.

As soon as I was inside my door, I closed it quickly and leaned against it, my breathing erratic. In the last six months I had frequently seen Talon popping up out of nowhere wanting to talk to me, to ask me what my plans were, and every time I acted like a freaked-out teen whose boy crush had just spoken to her.

No matter how my body wanted to jump his bones and get jiggy with him, my mind stayed strong and reminded myself that a relationship came with too much trouble.

At least that was what I kept telling myself.

"ZARA?"

I blinked back into the now and answered, "I—ah. No, I don't think. I mean, I'm not good company, and I have a friend coming over—"

"That's fine, just means we'll have to be quick." He winked.

Rolling my eyes, I walked off, but not before he

slapped me on the behind and then strode past me laughing.

I grumbled under my breath all the way up the steps, ignoring the other bikers across the road at the compound laughing, yet again, at me.

TWO HOURS LATER, I'd had a bath and gotten into my pink-with-black-kittens flannel PJs. Deanna texted an hour ago saying, *Hey, twat head. Not sure if I can make it. I'll let you know.*

So I sat down at my small, four-seater wooden table by the kitchen's large bay windows to eat my reheated Chinese. I had always found that Chinese tasted better when reheated.

Only then the doorbell sang. *Maybe Deanna made it after all.* I walked through my small lounge, which was furnished with a floral couch and one chair. A television sat on a long black unit against the wall, and a wooden chest acted as a coffee table in the centre. Nothing matched and that was the way I liked it. I'd saved and bought all of it myself, so I loved every piece of furniture in my house. I smiled before opening the front door.

"Kitten," Talon said as he looked at me from top to bottom. With a grin, he moved fast, because the next thing I knew, he was kissing me. My eyes sprang wide when his hot mouth touched mine.

"Talon," I mumbled around his lips, trying to shove him back. Unfortunately, well, not really, but still, yes unfortunately, when I spoke it gave Talon's tongue the chance to sneak in. As soon as it hit mine, I melted on a moan of abso-freakin'-lute pleasure. My abdomen clenched and my nether region quivered. I wrapped my arms around his neck and gave back as good as I was getting. In return, I received a groan. He picked me up, stepped inside, and kicked the front door closed behind him.

Holy crap, Talon's kissing me. ME. God, he is good. Wait, why is he kissing me? ME?

"Hot damn. I need some popcorn for this," I heard my best friend say.

I pulled away. My arms dropped to my sides, and he let me take a step back. Both of us were breathing hard. I took another step back, looked over Talon's shoulder, and found Deanna, smiling hugely, standing in the doorway with her hand still on the doorknob.

"Girl, you said he was fine, but you didn't say he was fucking F.I.N.E."

Talon raised his eyebrows at me and turned to face Deanna, in all his tight jeans and white tee glory.

"I-I've never said anything," I muttered.

"Hey, Talon. I'm Deanna, Zara's best mate. I've been

waiting for a glance of you for two fucking years. Oh, and I'm the one who will whip out some whoop-ass on you if you fuck her over, biker dude or not," she said in a pleasant tone, and then smiled sweetly.

Talon surprisingly didn't laugh. He looked her over and looked back at me. I knew what was running through his mind. Deanna and I were complete opposites. I was on the short side, had curves and lightly tanned skin from my Mexican background. I was sure Talon had the same sort of mix in his blood, only his skin was a little more like cocoa with a dollop of milk.

I had long, wavy, dark brown hair, and dark, forest-green eyes. Deanna was tall, thin, and was lucky enough to have been bestowed with a great rack. She had blonde hair, sky-blue eyes, and freckles on her nose to make her look that much cuter. She also had a big case of attitude. Though, it was all a front, of course. We'd both been through our own personal hell. We were just lucky to have found each other at the end.

"Nice to meet you, Deanna, and you have nothing to worry about," Talon replied.

What does that mean?

Deanna glared at him for a moment and then smiled. I felt, for a second, a pang of jealousy. Her smile had been the end of many men over the years, and right now, in her black pants and hugging tee that read 'watch 'em bounce' she looked great.

"I better not. Alrighty, wait till I get some popcorn and you two can continue what you were doing." She clapped her hands together.

"Uh, no. We can't. That—nuh-uh,"—I shook my head—"shouldn't have happened." My mind was in a whirl of thoughts.

Talon turned to me and said calmly, "It's been a hell of a long time coming."

"Wh-what?" I shook my head again.

"Come on, Zara, give the shmuck a chance. Then at least if it doesn't work out, I get to kick his bad-boy biker arse. A cute one at that; right again, lovey." She nodded at me.

I glared at my *ex*-best friend. "I have never said anything about his behind. Deanna, a word in the kitchen." I gestured with my head. Then I looked at Talon. "Uh, maybe you should go."

"I think I'll stay, kitten." He grinned and made his way to the couch. He sat down and propped his feet up on my chest—the wooden one—and turned on the TV.

I pulled the smiling Deanna down the hall, into my bedroom, and closed the door. Then I frantically got changed into jeans and a tee. Talon had already seen me in my PJs once, and that was once too many.

I spun to Deanna, put my hands on my hips, and glowered at her as she sat on my bed grinning.

"Oh, don't start. You need to live a little, girl. And I think biker boy can help you along the way."

"Deanna," I hissed. "I see nothing but danger with him around; and for God's sake, I am nowhere near his type. Look at me," I said, waving my hands up and down my body.

"And?" Deanna asked while looking at me like I was a loon.

"I have hips, I have a pudding belly, and I have dark brown hair. Not blonde and skinny, like he's always with, and have seen leave his place, and… Jesus, what the hell am I explaining myself for? There's danger all around him. Danger, Deanna. I can't go back to that. You'd have a better chance with him. Not that I want one."

She ignored my last statement. "You sound like that fucked-up robot off... shit, what's that show you like?"

"*Lost in Space*."

"That's it." She took a deep breath. "Zee, hun, you don't know that. Sure he's a badarse, but he ain't nothing like that other jerk-off. Nothing."

I threw my hands up in the air. "*You* don't know that. I have to think of Maya. She's my number-one priority."

"What about you, though? When will you let yourself be happy?"

"I'll wait till Maya's twenty. Then I can think about myself," I said, and crossed my arms over my chest.

"I bet—" Deanna was cut off by a knock on the front door.

I looked at Deanna and raised my eyebrows. I didn't know why, maybe I thought she magically knew who was at the front door. She shrugged, and then we both heard Talon growl, "Who the fuck are you?"

We bolted from my bedroom and ran down the hall. Coming into the living room, I focused on who was at the front door.

Oh, hell.

"Um, hi, Michael." I waved over Talon's shoulder because he hadn't moved from the doorway. He still held the door with one hand, as if he were ready to shut it on Maya's teacher from last year's face.

"Hi, Zara." Michael smiled.

"What are you doing here?" I asked, and tried to open the door wider to get it from Talon's grip. But he wouldn't budge, so I gave up.

Michael produced a bunch of wildflowers from behind his back. "I saw these and thought of you."

"She doesn't want them," Talon said.

"Talon!" I scolded.

"And who are you?" Michael asked.

"Her man."

I coughed and sputtered. "Ah, no you're not."

"Hot damn," I heard in the background from Deanna.

"Yes. I am." He turned to me, his form blocking my view of outside and Michael.

I put my hands on my hips. "Since when?" I glared.

"Kitten." He smiled. "Since I stuck my tongue down your throat and you curled your body around mine, moaning for more."

I was sure my eyes popped out of my head and walked off, then skipped with my heart down the path.

"Hot-double-damn!" Deanna laughed. "You'll have to give her a minute. Sorry, Mike. I think you're about ten seconds too late."

Talon shut the door in his face, which broke me out of my trance.

"Goddamn it, Talon. That was rude. And I am not your woman!" I opened the door and stomped down the front steps after a retreating Michael.

"Michael, I'm so sorry about that Neanderthal. That was very sweet of you to bring me flowers." Though, I didn't understand why since I'd told him "no" fifty times already when he'd asked me out.

"Don't ever do it again," Talon warned from the front porch.

I glared up at him. He winked and smiled down at me.

"I can see I've come at the wrong time. Maybe I should come back?" Michael asked.

"Uh..." was my response.

"No," came from Talon.

"I wouldn't bother," from Deanna.

I turned to them and sliced across my neck with my finger. Really, I was prepared to kill the both of them.

Spinning back to Michael, I smiled. "I'm sorry, Michael, but right now, at this time, I'm not ready for anything—"

A scoff came from Talon.

I continued, "The thought was very sweet, and I think you're a great guy—" God, I hated doing this; I always felt bad. Especially with a guy who was still holding flowers for me. "And you never know, maybe in the future—"

"Try never," Talon growled.

"Ever." Deanna giggled.

I winced. What was with the running commentary from the loco-train people? "Sorry, Michael."

"That's okay, Zara. I'll come back in a couple of weeks, see how things are."

I stopped myself from rolling my eyes. *Is that the future?*

"You come back, I'll kill you." Talon started moving from the front porch toward us. I quickly ushered Michael out the front gate and closed it.

"Everything okay, boss?" Griz asked. Griz was short for Grizzly, his biker nickname because he was built like a bear, in a cuddly sort of way. Not that he had a belly; he didn't. He was just tall, with very wide shoulders, arms, and legs. Griz was stalking across the street toward us.

Two others, whom I hadn't met, were standing on the other side of the road, legs apart, arms folded across their chests, looking menacing. I'd only met Griz because he helped me one day when I was attacking my lawn mower with a sledgehammer when it wouldn't start. He'd jogged across with an amused expression and asked, "Can I help, lady?" I let him, of course, or I'd be in jail right now for murder. I would have found a gun somehow.

I saw Michael studying Griz who was in his full motorcycle ensemble, including his black leather vest with a Hawks patch sewn onto it, their club's name.

"Y-y-you're a member of Hawks," Michael stuttered.

Griz stopped beside Michael and stared down at him. "Yeah, what of it?" he snapped.

"N-nothing." Michael turned back to Talon. "He, he called you 'boss.'"

Talon grinned his wicked grin and I grabbed the fence for support as Talon said, "Heard that, did ya?"

"Um." He looked to the ground. "Zara, I don't think I'll be back. Bye." He quickly marched off to his car. I was surprised his car didn't fly off, squealing down the road.

Deanna burst out laughing and walked toward us.

I sighed and ignored Talon's presence beside me. Instead, I turned my attention to Griz. "Hi, Griz. How's things?" He looked from me to Talon and then back.

"Great, Wildcat, and you?" He smirked. Wildcat had become my nickname from all the bikers since that first night. For some strange reason, no one else was allowed to call me kitten except Talon.

"Fine." I rolled my eyes and watched as the other two bikers disappeared into the compound.

"Now that's what I call entertaining. Girl, I gotta come to your house more often." Deanna grinned.

"Deanna, I think from now on I'm going to be a regular visitor at *your* place." *Just like I have been.*

"Kitten—" Talon began with a tone of warning.

"Pfft. Don't you 'kitten' me," I said with my back to him. He slipped his arms around my waist and pulled me close against his front. I held off a sigh of pleasure and tried to move away. It was impossible. I looked over my shoulder at him and bit my tongue to hold the moan. He looked gorgeous, even though his eyes told me he was annoyed. Still, they were laced with a little bit of lust as well.

Griz laughed but covered it with a cough when Talon glared at him.

"Oh, girly, we need to celebrate this. Let's get drunk," Deanna said. "Lord knows I need it."

I doubted I was supposed to hear that. I looked over at her and knew she was hiding something from me, but what was the mystery?

"And what are we celebrating exactly?"

"You and Talon gettin' it on." She gave me the *duh* look.

I went to move again but didn't get anywhere. "Uh, no. There is no Talon and Zara."

"Uh-huh." She smiled and looked at us from top to bottom. Okay, so to some it could seem different. Because I may have relaxed against Talon's warm, hot weight and my arms may be... okay, were resting on top of his, which were still wrapped around my waist.

Holy crap, I'm in Talon's arms.

He moved an arm from around me and swept my hair aside, then kissed my neck, which involuntarily arched so he could have better access.

Holy cow, Talon's kissing my neck. In front of people.

That didn't help my side of things. I nudged his head away with my own, and with some force, wiggled my way from his—wanted…so much needed…No!—unwanted and unneeded comfort.

I made my escape to Deanna's side.

Oh, my God, is my breathing heavy again? Yes, yes it is. Damn him and his sinful body.

"You"—I pointed my finger at him and glared—"stay over there. This"—I gestured between the two of us —"can't happen."

Deanna scoffed. Griz laughed.

"Kitten, I know you want me. Your body doesn't lie. It's only a matter of time before I'll be in your pants…" He trailed off as Griz's phone rang.

Griz flipped it open. "Yo? Yep." He closed it and looked at Talon. "Business, boss. Later, ladies."

"Bye, Griz." I smiled. It wasn't his fault his boss was a chauvinist arse-hat.

"See ya, hot stuff," Deanna purred, causing Griz to look over his shoulder, confused. He didn't understand that Deanna was attracted to older men, and Griz was definitely older. Deanna and I both sat at twenty-six. My guess, Talon was mid-to-late thirties, and Griz, with his long, muddy-brown-with-grey hair, and hard-aged eyes seemed to be hitting early forties.

"Kitten, I have to go. But if you two are having drinks, why don't you come by the compound later. I'll have a couple with you." With that, he grabbed my chin, kissed me hard and quickly, before my knee had the chance to hit his groin, and left.

Of course, I watched his fine arse walk away, and I was sure he knew it.

"Yeah, you keep fighting that, hun." Deanna laughed and walked into the house.

CHAPTER TWO

I followed Deanna back inside and reheated my Chinese, again.

Who did he think he was informing people he was 'my man'? Yeah, right! And why would he want me? He wasn't making sense.

This has been a long time coming. My arse it had. I couldn't recall how many times I'd avoided him for that reason alone. I was not some conquer-and-move-on type of girl if that was what he thought. And that was exactly what he'd want. I'd lost count of how many women I'd seen leave his place in the early hours of the morning. All blonde, I might add.

Though… it had been a while since the last one. Still, that didn't matter. The man was a tart when it came to women.

Urrh! I just wanted to scream.

"You're thinking too hard. Here, drink this," Deanna said and placed a glass of wine in front of me.

I turned a glare on her as she sat across the table from me and continued to roll her food around her plate.

I tipped my head to the side to study her. She'd never played with her food before. Usually, she'd have it gone in a second. And she never put on weight. *Bitch.*

"Stop lookin' at me like that. I will not fuck you, no matter how much you beg."

I snorted. God, I loved her. She was the only one who'd kept me somewhat sane through my two years of hell with David. I prayed every day he wouldn't know where to start looking to find me. I hadn't seen him in almost six years. So, my guess was we were just too good at disappearing a state away to the small town of Ballarat, where Deanna's other house was, or something had delayed his search for me. His business always did come first.

Still, I knew he would be looking for me eventually, because he didn't like to let go of possessions, and I was one. I'd hate to think where I would be, what I'd have put Maya through if I were still there. Deanna meant more to me than she could ever know. Which was why I was worried about her now.

"Tell me what's going on."

"Nothin'," she clipped and took a sip of her wine. A

second later, she drained the rest of her glass. One problem with Deanna was that she was as stubborn as a mule. If she weren't ready to talk about what was obviously on her mind, she wouldn't, leaving me to be the stress-head that I was and fret about it.

"Let's talk about Talon." She grinned.

"Let's not and have a drink instead," I said, and then drained my glass.

"I'll drink to that." She moved from the table to grab the bottle of wine but turned back around. "We're gonna need more than this. Where's your stash, woman?"

It was my turn to grin. She knew me too well. "The bourbon is in the laundry room, top cupboard." I needed something on those nights when I was about ready to hog-tie my brat of a child to her bed. Which I was sure every parrrenttt felt at one point in time or more.

A COUPLE OF HOURS LATER, I was feeling fabulous. We were dancing around the living room to Pink's "Fun House." Nothing was bothering me, and I could see that Deanna was having just as much fun as I was.

Then Deanna dumped her skinny behind on the couch, grabbed the remote, and turned down the tunes. At first, I was going to complain, but then I realised I was the verge of peeing myself.

"If you could be any superhero, who would you choose?" I called from the bathroom down the hall.

"What the fuck did you just say?"

Okay, so maybe it didn't come out like I thought it had. It could have sounded something like, "You be suuperaro what you chooose?"

"Ya heard me," I said while washing my hands.

"I think it's cut-off time, cocksucker."

I met Deanna in the kitchen, where she handed me a glass of water, and I drank every drop.

"I'd be Batgirl."

"Hah, knew'd ya heard. Me be..."

"Wonder Wanker."

I sprayed my second glass of water all over the floor, choked on my laughter, and gasped for air.

As I cleared my throat, a thought popped into my head, so I had to share it. "Oh, oh, I have one for Talon. Perfect Pecker Man." We both cracked up. Not that I'd seen his pecker, but I was sure it would be perfect.

Two more glasses of water later, and many more made-up hero names, I still felt a little foggy, but at least my speech had improved. Well, I thought it had.

"Man, I'm so glad I came over here tonight," Deanna said. Then there was a knock at the front door.

"You've still got time to take it back. Who the heck is that?"

"How many times do I have to tell you I can't see

through things?" Deanna teased as she followed me to the front door.

Deanna started bouncing from one foot to the other. I asked, "Do you have to pee? Or are you having one of those spontaneous orgasms you keep telling me about that I don't believe in?"

"No, no. None of that, and it is true, jealous whore, happened a couple of times anyway. But I just have a thought on who it'd be. Come on, open the fucker. I need some excitement."

I had a feeling too, but I hoped it wasn't. Me, plus drinks, plus Talon equalled something that should not be mixed.

Unlocking the door and swinging it open, I realised I should have hoped a little harder. Talon stood there looking spunky in dark jeans, a black tee, and motorcycle boots. His hair looked wet from a recent shower, and I wondered if I could blow-dry it for him with my mouth. My traitorous heart leaped, my body tingled, and…what the frig? How'd my underwear get wet already? Wait, had I peed myself? I looked down at the floor. Nope, wasn't wet.

That meant only one thing. "I need to get laid or break out my Gold Finger on maximum speed."

Deanna burst out laughing, and Talon seemed smug. I looked at them both, confused. *Oh, hell no.* I did not just say that aloud. See! Drinks, Talon, and me. It was a no-go!

"I could be of some help, kitten. In either way," he purred.

Or was that me purring?

I closed my eyes. My head fell forward, and I shook it from side to side. I was ready to die.

Deanna was going to be of no assistance; she was rolling around on the floor still laughing, so I asked, "Did you come over for a reason, Talon?"

"You're supposed to be at the compound, drinking."

I glanced up with my head cocked to the side. "What?"

He stepped closer. "Drinking. Compound. Now."

Straightening up, I glared and informed him, "No."

He took one step closer again, so he was flush against me. "What?"

"Did. I. Stutter?"

Something flared in his eyes, while something flared in my womb. Trouble was a-comin'. Talon bent his upper body level with my belly, and then he leaned in so I was flopped over his shoulder.

"Go, PP Man," Deanna shouted. She got up from the floor and followed Talon like a trained horny dog, out the front door and down the path. Thankfully, she had enough sense to shut the door behind us.

"Shut up." I glared at Deanna. "Talon... Talon put me down, now!" I ordered.

We'd made it to the gate when I heard new movement. Talon placed on my feet and pushed me behind him.

"Who the fuck are you?" he growled, and then looked over his shoulder. "Don't tell me you have another admirer."

"Um."

"Um? How fuckin' many do you have?"

"Um."

"Jesus Christ." His attention went back to the new arrival. "Again, who the fuck are you?"

"Zara?"

I gasped. I hadn't heard that voice in many years. "Mattie?" I looked over Talon's shoulder to see my now twenty-year-old brother, Matthew Alexander.

"Mattie," I cried, and flung myself at him. He wrapped me up in his arms and held on tightly. Though, it wasn't tight enough, because the next thing I knew, I was pulled away.

I glanced up and around to see Talon's fierce glare at my brother. I patted his hand at my waist. "It's fine; he's my brother."

"What's he doin' here? I haven't seen him before."

That was true. I looked back at my brother, and that was when I really took in what was in front of me. Instead of the free, fun-loving brother I was used to seeing in my mind, I saw a dirty, tired, worried and sad one. How had he found me? I left my family behind to keep them safe.

I stepped back farther into Talon's arms. "What's happened?" His face saddened in a way I didn't think was possible. "No, no. Don't tell me. I can't...no."

"They're dead, Zee."

"No!" If it weren't for Talon holding me, I would have crumpled to the ground. Deanna came to my side and grabbed my hand.

It couldn't be true. I'd only just finished planning a trip to meet my parents in Melbourne. They were to meet Maya for the first time. They were excited; I could see how much through the emails I'd sent them and Skyping with them.

I was excited.

Oh, God.

"It was a car accident. They say it was a freak accident."

My body shook; I felt cold and empty, I looked through my teary eyes. "Y-you don't believe that."

He shook his head.

Shit! It was him. I just knew it. It was David.

Snapping my emotions off, I stood tall. I had to go. Get away. Maya needed to be safe. She was what was most important.

Everything else could wait. My pain and heartache could wait... it had to wait. I needed Maya safe.

"Zee?" Deanna whispered. She knew what I was thinking.

I pushed away from Talon and started back to my house. I spun around to see the three of them following me. My gaze flicked across Talon on the phone and Deanna's worried look, until I settled on my brother.

Clearing my throat, I asked, "Were you followed?" He was unsure; I could see it. "Fuck, Mattie, were you followed?"

"I don't know." He looked at the ground. "I don't think so. I was careful, Zee."

Fuck! I couldn't risk it. I couldn't.

"Kitten."

Even when everything inside of me screamed to cry, to mourn for my beautiful parents, I didn't. I wanted to, I so wanted to, but I didn't. Stomping up the front steps, I flung the door open. I went to the kitchen and grabbed garbage bags, walked to the living room, and started bagging some of Maya's toys from her bin in the corner while wiping away the tears still falling; they just wouldn't listen to me when I said stop.

"Kitten?"

"I have to go," I uttered. "I have to get out of here. Shit, Maya's at school for her sleepover. That's all right; I'll get her. Mattie, you'll come with me. I can't lose you too—" I broke off on a sob. "How did you find me, Mattie?" I glanced over my shoulder to see him staring at me in shock and pain.

He shook his head. "You told mum the address." My eyes widened. Mattie went on, "No, she never wrote it down as you instructed. But she ended up telling me in case anything... happened to them."

There was a knock at the door. I screamed and dove for the couch. "Get down, get down," I whisper-yelled to Deanna and Mattie.

"Kitten, it's for me," Talon said and answered the door to Griz and three other bikers. They walked in, stopped, and closed the door. They took in what surrounded them and then focused on Talon, waiting. For what, I wasn't sure.

"I have to go," I whispered. I wanted to get up, pack the rest of my stuff, and flee into the night. But something held me there; my mind was reeling with unwanted thoughts. I was scared. So scared and hurting. My chest wouldn't stop aching.

"My parents are dead."

Mattie and Deanna moved toward me. I saw tears in Deanna's eyes. She never got teary. She was tough. Before they could get to me though, Talon moved in their way and knelt in front of me.

"Kitten. I'm sorry."

"Don't say that," I snapped. "You never met them. You could have, maybe one day... but now... I have to go. I have to move before *he* finds me." With a shaky hand, I reached out to his face and ran the back of my fingers over his unshaven cheek. "I'll miss you. I think. No, I will. We won't get to… you know. I think I would have enjoyed it." God, what was I saying?

Soft laughter started behind me.

Talon smiled. God, he was hot. "There's no thinkin' there, kitten. I'll rock your world."

"Maybe so. But not now, because I have to go." More tears fell from my eyes. My heart clenched tightly. "They're gone, Talon."

"I know, sweetheart."

"I have to go."

"You aren't fucking moving," Deanna shouted.

Suddenly, I found myself standing with my hands on my hips, facing her. Deanna stood in the same position on the other side of the couch. Anger fuelled my words. Anger was better than pain. "I have to. You know this, Deanna. You, of all people, know this," I yelled.

"Blah fuckin' blah. You ain't movin'. If he comes, we'll take care of it. I'm sick of you being scared." She pointed at me. "I hate seeing you always checkin' your doors, always looking over your shoulder. You will never move on and root hot pecker boy there and live your fuckin' life so you can be happy." She took a deep breath. "I'm sick of our past shit catching up," she said.

"Screw you!" I screamed, but blanched, my hand going

over my mouth. I had never screamed like that. I had never spoken like that to Deanna. I was losing it. But my apology was lost because next Deanna jumped over the couch and tackled me to the floor.

"Holy shit," I heard Mattie say.

While we rolled around, I kept trying to make my point, all sanity went when Deanna pulled my hair. "He'll come. He'll come and kill everyone I love. He'll take Maya and me away. We'll suffer for the rest of our lives."

"Not gonna fuckin' happen," Deanna hissed.

"Griz," Talon growled. Then I was lifted up and held against a muscular chest, as was Deanna, only she was struggling against Griz's grip on her. She didn't have a chance; and because she was pissed, she was missing out on the feel of Griz against her, which would probably piss her off even more.

"I will not let him hurt you. I'll kill him first," she said. "You know I will."

"I can't risk it, Deanna." I cried. "I'm more worried what he'll do to you, to Maya, Mattie and—" I looked over my shoulder at Talon, who seemed angry about something. "I won't let any harm come to any of you; and if *I* can stop that by leaving, I will do it."

"The fuck you will," she sneered.

"Yeah? I get it, Deanna. I get you're some tough bitch. You think you can take him, but I won't let you. I need you around. I care about you too much."

"Care on this." She gave me the finger.

"Screw. You. Again." I glared. God, were we acting like juvenile girls. Shame burned low in my belly, letting fear override any rational thoughts.

Deanna said nothing, but I saw in her eyes the same fear. We were *it* for each other, had been for so long. She didn't want to lose me like I didn't her.

"Holy fuck, boss! They're both wildcats," one guy said from near the door.

"Enough!" Talon snapped, and something in his tone made Deanna and me pause our argument. "Both of you shut the fuck up."

"Eat—" Deanna was about to swear until Griz placed his hand over her mouth and whispered something in her ear. Her eyes widened; he took his hand away and stepped back.

I turned in Talon's arms and glowered at him. "Don't you dare tell me to shut up."

"I will if you're an idiot."

I didn't like being called an idiot. It was too close to home. I had been an idiot staying with David. So, feeling fired with anger, I went to punch Talon; he dodged it and grabbed me around the waist, blocking my arms at my sides.

"Do that again, and there will be consequences."

"Yeah, like what?"

He moved his lips to my ear and whispered, "My

tongue in your mouth; my hand down your pants in front of everyone, and still, you'll enjoy it."

I gulped. How was I contemplating what he said when only seconds ago I'd been upset, scared, angry, and annoyed.

He pulled back and looked down at my face. What he saw made him smile. "Yeah, just what I thought." He pointed to the couch. "Now sit the fuck down, both of you, and start explaining."

My brain must have shut down, I sat and listened to him without saying anything back.

CHAPTER THREE

Damn him and his hot bossy words.

Was he right? Had this—us—been a long time coming? All those morning glances, teasing words and flaming wild wet dreams.

I guess it had. But the thing was—it was too late. Now I had to leave, to stay safe and keep others protected.

Which, at the end of it all, could be good for me, as it'd also keep my heart in one piece.

I wanted to hurl, to chuck my guts up. I wanted to cry, scream, and have sex.

Wait, what?

Could anyone make sense of that? Because I couldn't.

My heart and stomach clenched.

Oh, God...my parents.

Maya.

Deanna.

Mattie.

Smoking hot Talon

I placed my head in my hands and shook it. What was wrong with me? Why was I also thinking of Talon when my heart felt as though it'd been torn from my body with thoughts of my parents? Maybe I was losing my ever-loving mind. I was no longer sane. Yes, that had to be it. Well, it was either that, or I was dreaming. If so, what a stuffed-up dream!

"Kitten."

Nope. Not dreaming.

I peeked out of one eye, which brought me face to face with Talon's jean-clad perfect pecker.

Shit!

"You—" I sat up straight and pointed at him. "—you need to leave. You're a distraction, and I need to have a breakdown where I'll ugly cry, scream, and throw things." Or collapse in a heap and feel nothing but utter devastation.

Deanna snorted beside me. I'd forgotten she was there and that I had other company in the form of hot bikers.

"Kitten," Talon said again, with more of a growl.

Deanna sighed loudly and said, "Oh, for fuck's sake! Leave her alone. She's had some big shocks in such a small amount of time, and her pea brain is trying to handle it. Also, it doesn't help you standing there all manly, but whining at her like an old woman."

I loved Deanna!

So I told her just that. "I love you, Deanna."

She smiled. "Yeah, yeah. I'm all roses and chocolates and vibrators about you too, hun."

"Fuckin' hell. It's like talking to two deranged children." Talon glared at the both of us, causing laughter from the group near the front door.

"Hey," I snapped, a little late, even though I thought the same most times when Deanna and I got together.

"At least they're good-looking," one of the strippers commented—*bikers, Zara, bikers.*

I really must meet them all one day. Hold up—one day could never come. I sighed loudly to myself; at least I could be hospitable now.

I stood from the couch and faced them. "Sorry, guys. I should have asked this ages ago. Would anyone like a drink? Or, oh, what about a cookie? Everyone loves cookies. I can get more chairs too. I hate seeing people standing when I've been sitting my lard-arse down."

No one said anything; their gazes stayed fixed on Talon.

"We're fine."

I looked at Griz.

"Thanks," he added.

"Huh, I wouldn't have minded a cookie," the youngest and closest one uttered.

Well, at least I could make my brother more comfortable. I felt bad he'd been witness to all the craziness.

I turned to Mattie, who was sitting in a kitchen chair near the doorway, looking very confused, a little shocked, and a lot worried. "Mattie, what can I get you? You must be hungry? When was the last time you ate? I know, I can go set up the spare room bed."

Because it seems I won't be allowed to leave tonight.

Right! That was it. I stomped my foot because Mattie hadn't once looked at me; his gaze also fixed on Talon.

I spun back around to Talon. "You suck!" With my hands on my hips, I glared at him. My maturity had obviously left the building. Then again, I was sometimes a little different in the head than most.

He looked at the roof and sighed deeply. Probably praying for patience to deal with me. *Well, suffer in your tighty-whitey jocks, Talon.*

There was a knock at the door. A squeak escaped me and I went to dive for the couch, but a hand reached out and pulled me to a rock-solid body. Talon wrapped his arms around me and nodded to...

"Pick, open it," Talon ordered.

Pick, with the shaved head, goatee, and pale blue eyes nodded and turned to open the door.

I breathed a sigh of relief and unclenched my hands

from Talon's black tee when I spotted Blue, the only other member I knew of Talon's men. He'd been kind enough to help me unload my car one day after I'd been crazy shopping with Deanna. He was the only other one I found it hard to not stare at. Anyone with a humming passage would cream their pants if Blue came at them with his big muscles, skintight shirts, black leather pants, and biker boots. To top the look off, he had longish blond hair, light green eyes, and a smile that made my panties want to fall off and follow him everywhere.

"What's doin', Blue?" Talon asked.

"Cody." That one word made Talon stiffen and suck in a breath.

A child around twelve with scruffy black hair and deep blue eyes popped his head around Blue and gave a wave. "Dad."

What. The. Heck?

"What's goin' on, Cody?"

"Mum's busy, so I came here. Not here, but to the compound, and Blue brought me here," he said in a whisper. He seemed really shy, averting his eyes from Talon to the floor and back again.

"Shit!" Talon spat.

"Hey." I slapped him on the stomach. "No swearing around kids. Hi, Cody." I waved, smiled and stepped around Talon. "I'm Zara. I live here with my six-year-old daughter, Maya. Only she's not home at the moment, but at her school for a sleepover."

Blue gently guided him farther into the house with a hand around the back of his neck, and then shut the door.

"Can I get you anything, sweetheart? Would you like a cookie? A drink—"

"A chair," Talon muttered. I glared over my shoulder at him as he smirked back. "We've been through this, kitten. No one wants anything."

I watched Cody's expression change from puzzled to shock in a second when Talon called me kitten.

"Shush, Talon. Stop being so dang bossy."

He laughed, wrapped his hand around my neck, and brought me nose-to-nose with him. "You know you like it," he growled.

I pushed at his chest. "Whatever." I sighed and rolled my eyes. *Yeah, all right. I kinda like it.*

"We have shit to talk about, kitten—"

"Damn, I mean dang it, Talon. Stop swearing."

"I've heard worse." That whisper came from Cody. It was then I realised Talon and I were having our conversation still with our noses touching. I whacked his hands away and turned back to Cody.

But then quickly spun back to Talon, and on my own growl, I said, "Yeah, mister. We do have things to talk about, and one would be why the frig I'm just finding out now you have a son."

Talon laughed and then whispered, "There are a lot of things we don't know about each other, kitten. I look forward to finding out *each* detail." He scanned my body from top to bottom.

I shook my head and felt the need to shake my soaking panties, but resisted and faced Cody once again.

Distractions were always good. It was what I needed right then. Something to keep my mind chugging along on a different lane. A lane where my world wasn't ending, where my parents were still alive, still happy.

"Now, where was I?" I asked. "Oh, yes. You may have heard worse, Cody, and if you hang out with Deanna for five seconds, I'm sure you'll learn way more than any child should." Laughter filled the room. "But the point is, sweetheart, in this house, there is no swearing from anyone!"

Well, when children are around, that is.

"Okay, ma'am."

Deanna burst out laughing.

"Cody, you can call me Zee. All my friends do."

He gave me a half smile and then stared at the floor.

Talon came to my side, one arm placed around my shoulders, and he leaned in and kissed my temple. "That'll do," he whispered, which sent shivers down my spine. And with the hand that left my shoulders, he patted my behind and walked to his son, replacing Blue's hand with his own.

"Kitten, I'll be back. Griz, stay here. Boys, with me, now." And with so many wonderful words—*not*—he walked to the front door, opened it, and left with all the boys but Griz.

"Bye, Cody. It was nice meeting you," I yelled before Blue winked at me and closed the door after him.

"Well, I'll be damned. What a fucked-up night," Deanna said as she stood from the couch and stretched. I caught Griz taking it all in, but when he saw me looking, he went into the kitchen.

"Come on, Mattie," Deanna said. "We'll sort out your bed in the spare room. And, Zee…" She came at me. I tensed, but she hugged me instead. "Get the fuck into bed, hun. You look awful. I'll be in soon."

I nodded against her shoulder. She knew me. She knew I wanted to crash and burn. I needed my breakdown, and she was giving me the opportunity for it. Before I did though, I walked over to a quiet Mattie and pulled him against me.

"I'm sorry. So, so sorry that it took this to bring us together again. I love you, Mattie, and I'm glad you're here."

"So am I, sis, and they would be too. They'd be happy, darl', to know you're being taken care of. Even if they are a bit full on."

I laughed on a sob, kissed his cheek, and walked off to my room.

With the door closed, and without undressing, I fell to my bed and cried my soul out. I let it all free from its dark deep place within me. I let the pain out, the deep grief of no longer having my crazy but loving parents on this earth. The loss I felt was overpowering. It hurt in so many places: my head, body, spirit, but most of all my heart. It ached in a way I didn't think I could get over, but I knew I had to because of my precious little girl. And my parents would know that, they would understand why I was giving myself just that night to mourn the loss of them. Come tomorrow, I had many things to do; first of all was to get Maya to safety.

SOMETIME LATER, I was still in shattered pieces when I heard the door open. I didn't bother looking up. I knew it would be Deanna. I heard shoes hit the floor, harder than Deanna would treat her precious pumps, but thought nothing of it until a solid, hard warmth hit my back. Unless Deanna had morphed into a male, it definitely wasn't her.

"Jesus, kitten. I'm sorry, Zara. I should have been back sooner." Talon's breath ran across my neck, and then he kissed it.

His sweetness made me want to cry harder. “D-don’t. I can’t handle you being n-nice. Be an arse, please.”

He chuckled and pulled my back flush against his front. “All right, kitten. Wanna fuck?”

I snorted and wiped away my fallen tears. “Dick.”

“Wench.”

I sighed and snuggled in closer. “I’m scared, Talon.” So very scared and hurt.

“I know. But, as words spoken from Deanna, you ain’t fuckin’ leavin’,” he growled. “We’ll get through this.”

And that was what also scared me—the ‘we’ll’ part. He’d placed himself in there with me. Was I ready for that? Hell no.

But as sleep started to take me, I felt protected.

“Keep your perfect pecker to yourself.”

I heard another rumble of laughter before I drifted off.

CHAPTER FOUR

I did not want to get up and face the day. Could it be possible that no one would notice my absence? Doubtful. I still had to get to work, pick Maya up, and fly the coop without any problems. Just the thought made me groan. I knew it wasn't going to be easy. Problems were bound to come my way.

Problem one, the most important one: the fact I had to bury the loss of my parents for now while I skipped town and got my daughter and brother to safety. My heart didn't want that. It still wanted to roll over and cry.

Problem two: whenever I closed my eyes, all I pictured was Talon in my bed. I turned my head to see that spot now empty. It was probably for the best. I wouldn't have been able to control myself as I had through the night. When I woke, and he was holding me tightly against him, other than feeling like I was being smothered, it felt nice. Then I realised where one of his hands was. Cupping my sex. Of course, I had to wriggle a little, only I shouldn't have because it sent a pulse of lust throughout my body and I so wanted to do it again. My first thought was maybe he wouldn't notice if I accidentally got *off* from his hand. I wiggled again, holding back my moan, and that was when his shiver-worthy voice rumbled at the back of my neck.

"If you do that again, you'll see how perfect my pecker is."

I froze and damned him into a coma so I could continue with his hand. Unfortunately, it didn't work; so then I contemplated the thought of just using him for the night, to forget, and because I wouldn't be around much longer.

"Stop fucking thinkin'. The noise your brain makes is keeping me awake."

I settled back with a loud sigh, just to annoy him. Fine, if he was going to be an arse, I was going to keep my wet tunnel away from him.

Double fine, if he was going to be an arse about it and not move his hand, I was going to ignore it and sleep.

And I did.

Eventually.

Problem three: the voice I heard rise down the end of the hall in the kitchen. Who Deanna was yelling at, I had yet to figure out. I could only hope it wasn't my brother. I was sure Deanna's foul mouth could just about scare Satan himself.

Problem four: my bladder was screaming at me to get out of bed and deal with it.

I got up, peed, had a shower, and dressed in jeans, a red sweater, socks, and with my hair still damp, I walked out of my room.

On the way down the hall, I paused to listen in on the conversation being held in the kitchen.

"You fuckin' mean she doesn't work for that law firm anymore?" Talon asked.

Deanna snorted and said, "Turn up your hearing aid, old man, and listen carefully. No, she doesn't work there no more."

"Where she at now?"

"At some PI place not far from here."

"Hell. Please don't tell me *'We put the P in PI'*?" he asked with disgust in his voice.

"Yeah, I think that's it. Like I said, she hasn't been there long, two weeks tops."

"Fuck!"

I heard a bark of laughter that didn't sound anything like Talon or Deanna, so I guessed Griz was still here.

What was the big problem with where I worked?

I found Violet, Chuck, and Warden great people to

work with. It wasn't like I was doing any of the PI work. I was their secretary and that was it.

"Griz," Talon barked. *Ha, I'm right*. Griz's laughter died.

"Come on, boss. It'd have to be a co-winky-dink."

"I doubt it."

"A fuckin' what?" Deanna asked with a smile. I could hear it in her voice.

I peeked around the corner to see Griz stiffen and glare at her, and then he said, "A coincidence."

"Yeah, uh-huh." She raised one eyebrow.

For the first time, I turned my gaze to Talon, and I wished I hadn't.

He was leaning against the sink in jeans and—yes ladies, that was it! I got a full view of his stunning, bare...um, let's say feet. His chest wasn't that bad either. But what topped it off, what made me feel the need to fan my private area, again, was the tribal tattoo that covered his left shoulder, and then another tattoo on his right set of ribs of a fierce-looking dragon. Maybe I could haul him by the hair of his head to bed and have my wicked way with him.

Distractions were good.

No. That wasn't an option.

I had hoped to wake with no one to deal with, so then I'd have the chance to make a clean getaway. Of course, that would have been after I called work and explained that soon there'd be a madman after me, so I wouldn't be able to work there any longer because I'd be running for my life. Then I'd ask them if they wanted me to drop off some coffee and donuts on the way.

But no, yet another plan foiled.

Stupid, caring people.

Sighing, I stepped out from around the corner. "Morning all," I chirped and looked out the kitchen windows. "Oh, poop. It's drizzling outside." *Damn it, my stuff is going to get wet when transferring it from the house to the car.*

"Can't be helped," I added. "So, what's everyone doing today?" I asked while pouring myself a freshly brewed cup of coffee from the maker besides the sink.

"Either you did her last night and did her good, or she's high," Deanna said.

I wish. I could go for a bit of both.

"Deanna, hun. Whatever do you mean?" I turned to look at her.

"*Zee,* sweet chops, I know you."

"Huh? What's that got to do with anything? A-a-a-anyway, thanks for staying last night, but, uh, y'all better get going. Isn't there work to get to? And I got to get ready for mine. So, uh, thanks."

"And there we have our answer," Deanna said smugly, leaning back in her chair.

"What?" Talon asked. I still hadn't looked at him; my

eyes stayed on Deanna or the floor.

"She wants us gone so she has the chance to run and hide with her head up her arse."

I stiffened, my cup half raised to my lips. Stuff Deanna and her knowing me too well.

Talon's head fell back, and he let out a deep rumble of laughter, sending goosebumps all over my body.

He shook his head and then looked at me…no, I should've said glared at me. Hoo boy.

He pushed away from the sink and slowly, sensually, moved toward me. He took my cup from my hands and placed it on the bench behind me. Which gave me a chance to draw in a good whiff of him, causing my body to respond.

My hands went to his chest; his went to my waist. I looked up at him.

"Let's get one thing straight right now, kitten." I nodded. "I won't have you runnin'. This is your fuckin' place; nothing is runnin' you off. I won't fuckin' let it. You get me, woman?" This time I shook my head. He sighed. "Even though my dick ain't been in you—yet—I still classed you mine once my mouth touched yours. You have my protection, kitten. My boys' protection. Nothin' is gonna fuckin' happen to you, Maya, or Hell Mouth there."

"Thanks," Deanna grinned.

Wow! What was I supposed to say to that? Was he like

this for all his hoochie mamas? Not that I was his HM. We hadn't even slept together.

Still, no matter how his words made me feel, the urge to run and hide was stronger than anything else. Not only for my sake, but for Maya's, and to keep those who wanted to protect me safe.

"No."

His eyebrows rose. "What?" he said with a growl.

"I can't let you do that. I won't have any harm come to you and your boys because of me, and you can't ask that of them either. Promise, I'm really not that good of a lay."

He leaned his forehead against mine. "For fuck's sake, kitten." I could hear the smile in his voice.

"Too damned considerate," Deanna grumbled.

Griz stood abruptly. We all watched him leave the room and heard the front door slam seconds later.

"What's his problem?" Deanna asked.

"Nothin'," Talon said. He kissed me quickly—way too quickly if you asked me—stepped back, and said, "We got shit to talk about. Finish your coffee, babe, and then both of you get your arses in the living room." With that, he stalked out, down the hall, and no doubt into my room to use my en suite.

"I'm upset with you, bitch," Deanna said, crossing her arms over her chest.

"Yeah, well, I'm upset with you too, whore." I glared. "Why did you have to tell them what I was going to do?"

"'Cause I see the way PP man looks at you, and I knew he'd put a stop to your fucked-up plan." She got up from the table and came over. Deanna gently took my face between both her hands, holding my gaze with the strength of her own. "I can't lose you, woman. I'd be in a fuckin' mental home if it weren't for you. I need you to listen to me. You need to stay and fight. You have people willing to fight at your side with you, or for you for that fuckin' matter. Don't run. Please, please, don't run."

Tears formed in her eyes. I had never seen Deanna like this in all the years I'd known her.

I grabbed her in a tight hug, fighting my own tears. "Honey, you know that's not me. I can't have people fight my battles."

"We want to. If that's what'll keep you and Maya here, we will."

"I know *you* do. I know. And Talon, maybe. God only knows why. But Talon's boys?" I shook my head on her shoulder. "You know what dickface was like; if one of Talon's boys got hurt, or worse, because of me, I couldn't live with myself."

"Lounge, now," Talon's gruff voice ordered.

We pulled apart, wiping our faces, and saw Talon leaning against the doorframe. He had wet hair and wore jeans and a black tee. How long had he been there? I wasn't sure. But God almighty, he looked good enough to eat.

"I hate you," Deanna said to me before she left the room.

"And I hate you, too." I smiled at her back as I followed her into the lounge. Finally, I knew she understood.

We both sat on my couch. Talon grabbed a kitchen chair, dragging it in to sit opposite us across the wooden chest. The front door opened, scaring the crap out of me, nearly causing me to jump in Deanna's lap. Griz stomped back in, but it didn't stop there; about ten other bikers walked in behind him. They made themselves comfortable standing or sitting where they could, while Deanna and I stared with slack jaws.

What's going on?

"Man, I wish to fuck I had a shower now before this," Deanna grunted. I giggled. I would have felt the same way if I was still in the clothes I had on yesterday, and the massive bed hair she had going on. Still, she looked beautiful. The nut sucker.

"Kitten. Start explaining." It wasn't a question. It was an order.

"What? Now?"

He rolled his eyes. "Yes, now."

I looked around the room, wondering why Talon wanted me to tell my sob story in front of so many badarse bikers.

"*Kitten,*" Talon growled.

"All right, all right. You are damned bossy. Has anyone ever told you that?"

"All the time," he said. His boys laughed.

"Yeah, well, it'll only work on me so many times; in the end, you'll have no chance to get in my knickers." My hand flew to my mouth. I really just said that in front of people.

He smirked. The guys laughed again.

"I'm willing to think otherwise." He grinned, then it disappeared. "We don't have all day, babe. Some of us have to work."

I sat up straighter. "Speaking of which, I've got to call my boss. She'll be wondering where I am."

"Already done," Deanna said. I turned to her in time to see her shrug. "I said you wouldn't be in. She asked why. I told her to mind her own fuckin' business."

My hand went to my mouth again. "You didn't."

"She did," Griz said.

"Jesus, Deanna—" I started to tell her off good and proper, but there was a knock on the door.

"Better not be another fuckin' suitor," Talon said through clenched teeth.

Pick was the closest to the door and opened it. I saw Warden's tall form over everyone's heads. "I'm after Zara," Warden barked.

"Who the fuck are you?" Pick asked.

Talon stood, his fists clenched at his sides. I could read the look he was giving me: 'not another fuckin' one.'

"None of your damned business." Warden took a step forward and leaned down to get in Pick's face.

I stood quickly and waved over everyone. "Hey, Warden. Over here." Out the corner of my mouth, I whispered to Talon, "I work with him."

Warden stalked through the many bikers, came right up to me, and pulled me into a tight hug. I patted his back and then waved Talon off when I saw him approach.

"Get ya fuckin' hands off her," Talon growled.

Warden, being Warden, fazed by nothing because he was big enough to take on all of them, simply ignored Talon. He pulled back from the hug and gently grabbed my face between his palms, then said, "Looks like we made it here in time."

"We?"

"Violet's parking the car. She saw all the bikers comin' in and she told me to get my arse in here. Lucky I did. Now, what the hell's going on?"

"Shit!" Talon hissed. "You need to back the fuck up, or we're gonna have problems."

Warden stiffened. He removed his hands, turned, and placed me directly behind him. He was trying to protect me. *That's so sweet? My co-worker likes me and we haven't even been working together long.*

The front door swung open, and in it stood Violet in a

fighting stance, holding a gun to the room. She kinda looked funny, not that I would tell her that. She's tiny, not only short, but she's slim, with long black hair, which was always in a ponytail, and dark green eyes.

However she looked, I still knew not to mess with her. Honestly, it wouldn't surprise me if she shot someone and thought nothing of it.

"Who do I have to shoot first?"

See.

"Vi," Talon said in a low voice. On hearing it, Violet stiffened. Her eyes found him through the mountain of bikers—one that I wouldn't mind climbing—and she straightened.

"Brother." She sneered her contempt.

What was that? Did I hear right? I think I went deaf there for a second and my mind made up its own word. I stuck my finger in my ear and wiggled it.

My hand dropped when Violet walked into the room, kicked the door closed, holstered her gun, and strutted her way over to stand next to Warden.

"Really, Talon. I didn't expect you here. Zara's not your type—"

"That's what I said," I added.

"She's too good for you."

"Well, I don't know about that." I shrugged.

"What the fuck're you doing here?" Deanna asked from *still* sitting on the couch.

By all means, Deanna, don't get up. There's going to be one hell of a fight. All. Because. Of. Me. But just sit back and enjoy the show, Deanna. Want some popcorn?

"Well, Barbie, I knew something was up when you and your foul mouth called. I know Zara isn't one to not call herself. So I had to pop in and find out what was going on."

"And you thought it had something to do with me, right?" Talon glared.

"Couldn't be too careful. Imagine my surprise when Zara walked into my office one day asking for a job, and I just happened to see her address on her résumé. I knew it was fate. It was up to me to keep an eye on her—from the likes of you. But look-see here, you've already got your claws into her. Now tell me what's going on?"

"Violet—" I started.

"Kitten," Talon warned. I looked over to him; he shook his head and held his hand outstretched. "Come 'ere."

Damn, it was a test. Like those ones people put on dogs when one master stood on one side of the room and the other on the opposite side and they both called the dog to see which one was the favourite master. Actually, you know what? That was a bad example. I was not the dog in this scenario.

But I did feel I had to choose, and my gut, head, and heart only had one answer.

I stepped around Warden and made my way to Talon. I placed my hand in his; he pulled me tightly against his side with a smirk on his lips.

I punched him in the side. "Don't go all alpha on me and be a smart-arse. Violet, Warden, you may have different opinions of Talon, but he isn't all that bad. And now just finding out you're his sister, I'm sure you've got some stories to tell me." I leaned forward and whispered, "I look forward to hearing them and getting some dirt on him.

"And sure he's as bossy as a shithead sometimes, but you've got to look at his good side as well. Okay, it may be hard to find, and you have to really squint to see it, but it's there, and I kinda like it."

The room burst out laughing. Talon gripped my waist, so I looked up at him. He was smiling as he ran his knuckles down my cheek and then proceeded to kiss me in front of everyone. There were some hoots and hollers.

He took his lips away from mine, and I think I complained a bit, but then he whispered, "You'll pay for that shithead comment, kitten. And next time, do not say this crap in front of my boys. I'm a badarse motherfucker."

He straightened and announced to the room. "Let's get this shit sorted."

"We're staying," Violet said.

Talon gave her a chin lift and continued, "Kitten, sit

down and start explaining." Talon's phone rang. He answered it, and whatever he heard on the other end made his smile turn upside down because next he growled deeply, "Bring the fucker in."

CHAPTER FIVE

A few seconds later, the front door opened and the young cookie-liking biker walked in, closely followed by Blue. I was shocked to see Blue restraining a reluctant dark and handsome stranger.

"Blue?" I asked. Talon pulled me closer, both his arms wrapped around my waist.

Deanna stood up from the couch. "What's going on *now*? I don't mind the entertainment, but it's startin' to get a bit much." She turned her concerned eyes to me. I shook my head. This was as surprising to me as it was to her.

"Who the fuck are you and why are you hounding around this house?" Talon asked the shocked-looking guy.

Said guy gasped. "Holy Mother Mary, I've hit the

payload. No fucking wonder he deserted me to come here. The bastard. Where is he? I'm going to cut off his penis."

Blue shoved the guy hard, and he stumbled forward. It was obvious to everyone he wasn't a danger. Besides, if he did—which I doubted—try anything, the house was already full of mean-looking people who'd take him down. But it was also a sense that he wouldn't have the heart to hurt anyone.

He straightened, fixed his clothes on his lean body, turned to Blue, and glared. "Well, really. I like a bit of roughness, but only in bed, honey."

Blue snapped, "Fuck off."

I giggled. I couldn't help it. Blue turned a fierce glare on me, but my giggle also brought the attention of our guest.

"Well, spank me. You must be Zara." He smiled.

My eyes widened. Talon stepped in front of me and said, "You do not speak to her or look at her until you tell me who the fuck you are."

"Don't get your knickers in a bunch, love muffin." He looked over Talon's shoulder to me. "He is lickably-'licious, sweetheart."

"I think I love this guy," Deanna said.

He faced Deanna. "Thanks, doll, aren't you gorgeous too. I'm sure the feeling will be mutual."

"Fuck." Talon made a beeline for the guy, who started backing up quickly.

"Whoa, hold up, Hercules. I'm just making friends here."

"Tell me who the fuck you are or my fist—"

"Julian?" The room turned to see a startled Mattie.

Talon stopped his pursuit and stalked back to me. His arms wound around my middle again.

"Hell, I think I just soiled myself." Julian sighed.

"What are you doing here?" Mattie asked.

"Who is he?" Talon glared at Mattie.

"A... a friend."

"Seriously, dickface? You forgot the *boy* in front of that friend. Or is it because you've found your sister and a house full of Chippendales that I'm suddenly a memory?"

Mattie, with an outstretched hand, said, "No, no. It's nothing like that."

"Whatever." Julian harrumphed, crossed his arms over his chest, and ignored my brother's gaze.

"Oh, this is exciting." I smiled, wiggled my way out of Talon's hold, and walked over to Julian. "It's so nice to meet you." I hugged him. "Mattie only got here last night. I had a little breakdown, but I'm sure if that hadn't happened, he would have told me all about you."

"Well, aren't you just beautiful? Thank you, precious, and I'm so sorry for your loss. I understand Mattie wanting to find you and tell you himself, but to leave me behind? Nope." He shook his head. "That just doesn't jive with me." He leaned in and whispered, "I think he was worried how you'd take to him being gay." He stood straighter and smiled. "But you're handling it just fine and dandy. Now tell me, cupcake, how in God's name have you got a house full of orgasmic men?"

I grinned and pointed to Talon. "That one thinks he has some claim on me because he stuck his tongue in my mouth yesterday. He's their head honcho."

"Fuck me." Talon looked at the ceiling.

"I'll take you up on that, Iron Man," Julian said with a flutter of his eyelashes.

"Julian!" Mattie snapped. "Sorry! He's sorry. He didn't mean it."

"Christ, enough. What the hell am I thinkin'?" Talon asked.

I put my hands on my hips and glared at him. "I certainly don't know. But I can easily fix that and leave."

"Say or think that one more time, I'll take you to bed and fuck some sense into you."

Julian squeaked beside me. "He sounds serious."

I looked at Julian and rolled my eyes. "He probably is."

"Everyone shut it. We need this shit sorted."

"He's real bossy too," I said to Julian.

"*Kitten,*" Talon growled.

"All right, jeepers." I grabbed Julian's hand and led him

over to the couch. The silently watching Violet and Warden moved to stand near Talon, across from us.

Julian sat between Deanna and me, and Mattie breathed deeply and plopped himself on the edge of the couch.

"Hey, I'm Julian." He held his hand out to Deanna.

"Deanna." She gave him a chin lift.

"What's going down here?" Julian asked.

"Her PP man is waiting for an explanation on her past, and why she fuckin' wants to up and leave ever since Mattie found her."

Julian raised his hand, yelling, "Oh, oh. I know why. 'Cause her crazy ex, right?"

Deanna nodded and went on. "So now, the idiot keeps getting the thought in her pea brain head that it's best to just up and run to keep her and Maya safe as well as everyone else here."

I glared. "You don't get it. No one does. If he finds me, someone will end up getting hurt. I'm—"

"Woman." Everyone looked at Griz when he barked that one word. The other bikers who had been playing with their phones or quietly talking amongst themselves fell silent and stood straighter as if waiting for their cue. "That's why I left earlier. You may have a hard time coming to terms that you're Talon's woman, but once he claimed you, you became a part of Hawks. We take care of our own, and now, that means you. So don't fuck around with thinkin' and worrying 'bout us. We live for this shit. We'll protect you no matter what shit you dribble. Ain't that right, boys?"

A chorus of 'Fuck yeah', 'Damn straight', and wolf calls echoed through my tiny house, which brought tears to my eyes.

I held up one hand. "But—"

Griz interrupted and said, "Shut ya gob and go with it; nothing you say will change anything. Now get the fuck back to work."

I realised he wasn't talking to me when the bikers started to disappear out the front door. Only a few stayed: Griz, Blue, and Pick.

"Kitten, it's finally fuckin' time to sort this shit."

Me, being my stubborn self, shook my head. I thought if he didn't have the information, he couldn't go off half-cocked and get him and his boys hurt.

"Okay, if you ain't talkin', I will," Deanna yelled.

"Don't. You. Dare," I snapped.

Violet cleared her throat. "If she doesn't, I will. You need to stay safe. And against all my better judgment, I think my brother can do that."

"How do you know her shit?" Deanna snapped.

Vi wrinkled her nose, raising her upper lip. "Barbie, I'm a PI. Of course I did a check on her."

"You suck, just like your brother." I crossed my arms over my chest and slouched down in the couch acting a like a child, but I seriously didn't want my story retold, it was had enough living it, so hearing it wasn't up on my top choices of things to do that day.

"Just for that comment, I'll tell your whole frigging history."

"Violet!" I snapped.

"Nope." She shook her head.

"Someone just fuckin' start talkin'." Talon sighed. "Give me the info I need to keep my woman safe."

Vi took a breath and began, "Zara Edgingway was actually born Zara Alexander. She accidentally told me her last name when she came in, and I realised it was different from the one on her résumé. Zara grew up in Manly, NSW with her parents and her brother Matthew. She graduated high school. But then she met David Goodwill when she was working at Starbucks. He charmed her into believing he was a good, caring guy. They married young, but—"

I couldn't look at anyone. David had suckered me into his fairy tale, and now my whole life was being aired like some leather-fetish grandma.

"—unbeknownst to Zara, David Goodwill dealt with the mob on the side of his club business. He's also dabbled in drugs, selling women, and guns. He's one evil motherfucker."

Holy cow… I knew he was bad, but not like that.

"Why'd you leave him, Zara?"

Oh, that hurt. Not kitten, but Zara. I couldn't tell him the real reason. I was already Zara. If he really knew the truth, the filth, what would I become then? Nothing. So I shook my head and lied, "I found out what he did."

"Zee," Deanna uttered. I caught her gaze with my own pleading eyes. She sat back and said nothing.

Something shattered. I gasped and looked up to see that Talon had thrown a vase to the ground, one that had been near the television. "Don't fuckin' lie to me!"

"Talon," Blue barked.

"I'm not, and don't throw my stuff around," I said with my head held high.

"Two years I've waited for you to come to me. I've been waiting and watching, Zara. I know you. I know when you're angry, when you're sad, upset, worried, happy, horny, and fuckin' lyin'. Tell me the truth. Why did you leave him?"

My bottom lip trembled. Goddamn him for saying that shit to me. The arse wasn't allowed to say nice stuff. I was going to have to ban it from the house.

Though, this could work. If I told him, he'd move on. Let me go. It would hurt, but it'd be for the best.

And besides, nothing could hurt more at that moment than still feeling the loss of my parents.

Standing, I glared at him, my fists clenched at my sides, and yelled, "You honestly want to know? I'd had enough of his beatings. Something had changed in him.

He never hurt me until two months before I left. But what topped it off, what had me call Deanna in the middle of the night and escape, was when he came home drunk, beat me, and *then* raped me!" I pounded my chest.

Talon's hands were clenched; he was breathing deeply through his nose. My eyes widened as, what felt like, a mountain of rage filled the room. Griz quickly started issuing orders.

"Fuck! Deanna, take Zara to her room. Gay guys, PIs, go with them." Blue and Griz ran across the room and grabbed Talon's arms. "Go now," he growled.

Vi, Warden, and Mattie were already heading down the hall. Deanna grabbed my hand, Julian took the other one and dragged me along with them. We'd gotten my door shut before a roar of fury filled the house. "I'm gonna fucking kill that motherfucker! Let. Me. Go."

The boys must have let go because the next thing we heard were things being thrown around.

"Talon, get the fuck outside," Blue yelled.

We listened to the front door being snapped open, hitting the wall.

"Clean this shit. We'll calm him," Griz said to someone.

Moments later, the rumble of Harleys started and took off down the street.

"Well, honey, I think I can honestly say I have never seen this much action in all my life. I love it here. Mattie, we're moving." Julian smiled from where he sat next to me on the bed.

"That was fuckin'... wow. I have never seen a man that... super angry before. Hot or what?" Deanna gleamed with excitement. She was sitting on the other side of me.

Deanna and I both knew we'd seen others that angry before. However, this was a different situation. We knew that no harm would come from said super-angry person. It was actually funny how un-scared I was, especially with what my past had detailed. In fact, I was anything but scared. What I felt was nauseous and sad that I had upset Talon in any way.

"So hot I think I came in my pants. Sorry, honey," Julian said. Mattie smiled and nodded in agreement, then patted Julian's leg.

"Hot-frigging-headed. He's always been like that," Vi said, shaking her head. She and Warden were standing in front of the door.

"Maybe... maybe he'll leave me alone now," I uttered.

"Oh, here the fuck we go. Where is that mushed-up brain of yours leading you?" Deanna asked.

"Now he knows."

"What, Zara?" Mattie asked.

"He knows I'm not good for him. I'm filthy."

"Fuck," Warden hissed, opened the door and left.

"Too much girl talk for him, I'm guessing." Julian

smiled. "And Zara, my potato pie, from what I just witnessed and heard, Talon is far from done with you. You ain't filthy, girl. That pubic-hair-flossing ex of yours is as good as dead. You are much loved here, woman, and if it ain't you or Deanna or Talon doing the killing, you're going to have many others stepping forward to fulfil that job. That fucktard should never have laid a harmful hand on you. He's gonna pay, pop tart. No matter what you say. And Talon will be at your side through all this hell to come. Everyone can see the hard-on he has for you."

CHAPTER SIX

"All right, while my brother goes off to cool his jets, I need information. First, why are you so interested in running off half-baked? Which will probably get you into more trouble than before," Violet asked, looking almost as angry as Talon had.

"Someone could have followed Mattie. I need to get out of here before they show up, or the dickhead gets here himself," I said.

"Not that she's sure Mattie was followed. If anything, they would have followed Julian," Deanna said. "Fuck," she uttered when she saw my wide eyes of worry.

"You're safer here than anywhere else in the world. Talon will go to great lengths to keep you that way. As you can see and have heard a million times, Zara, it's not only him. I'm sure Barbie would as well. Then you have the guys and me."

I rolled my eyes. "That right there is why I have to go."

"You're scared. That's all it is. You're not thinking."

I bounced down to the end of the bed; there was a lot of jiggling going on, which must have looked like a treat. But I was pissed. I got up and in Violet's face.

"Of course I'm scared," I hissed. "If a man like that was after you, wouldn't you be? And I am thinking as straight as Talon in a gay bar."

Julian chuckled behind me. "I'd like to see that."

"Oh, no, no, in a gay strip club," Deanna added.

"Shh, you guys," Mattie ordered.

Vi glared and said, "No. You. Aren't. If you were, you'd know that this, staying here with us all, was the right choice. Not only the right choice for you but for Maya. Think, Zara. If you're out there on your own, running for your life, what are you going to tell Maya? How are you going to keep her safe? You'll be by yourself."

I teetered back. "I…I don't know."

"I understand the urge to run. I do. But it won't help. It's time to trust the people around you, to lean on them for help when they're so willing to do just that. No matter what may come of the situation."

I flopped back on the bed. Damn, she was right.

All I wanted was to run, to keep everyone safe, but I

hadn't been thinking clearly. Maya was the highest priority, and it hadn't dawned on me that she'd need more than just me to keep her protected from her cuckoo father. Even if the thought of having others involved in my stuffed-up situation still sent me into panic mode and wanting to sit in the corner sucking my thumb, I needed to stop, take a breath, and think.

I sat up straight and turned to Mattie. "You have to leave before things get ugly."

"*If*," Deanna said.

Mattie smiled. "We're family, and I've only just gotten you back in my life—"

Julian interrupted, "Oh, my Gawd, I'm gonna cry. This is one of those Hallmark moments." He sniffed.

Mattie rolled his eyes. "And I've had my fair share of ugly in my life, so I'm kind of used to it."

"You better not be referring to me, sac sucker."

Deanna laughed. "I love that one, sac sucker. I'm going to have to use it."

"Make sure to use it on a straight guy. Lordy, that would be funny."

Deanna turned to me. "So, you're staying?"

"Yeah."

"You're a fucking miracle worker, but I still don't like you." Deanna glared at Violet.

"And you think I care." She turned her bored gaze to

Julian. "I have a question for you, though. How'd you know Mattie was here?"

"I overheard the convo' he had with his mum about where his sister lived. I memorised the address as well."

"And you didn't tell me because..." Mattie's wild eyes told me he was a little annoyed by the fact Julian hadn't said anything.

"Oh, I knew one day you'd sneak off without telling me, on a mission to get to her, and not tell her where you preferred your dick to lay every night. Of course, I knew if I showed up, she'd love me, and in the end wouldn't judge you. Which is how it all worked out."

"Still, you should have informed me," Mattie mumbled.

"Your ex doesn't know anything about Maya, right?" Vi asked me as she moved away from the door.

"No, he doesn't," I said.

"That there is great news. Honestly, it's been this long, he's either given up or is too stupid to figure out where you are."

My door suddenly swung open, revealing Warden; his eyes met Violet's. "Done a sweep. Nothin' out there. Your bro already has men on the lookout." His eyes then fell on me. "Got his number from that wanker out there—"

"Fuck you," Pick yelled from the front room.

"Rang your man; told him what you said—"

"Warden!" I yelled.

"On ya, dude." Deanna laughed.

"Goodness," Julian breathed.

"Shit," Mattie uttered.

"He's on his way back." Just as he said that we heard the sexy rumble of the Harleys. My heart rate skyrocketed, and I was ready to run and hide in my closet. But for some reason, I thought the people in the room would have told him where I was.

Quickly scooting back down to the end of the bed where Deanna and Julian were sitting, I placed myself in the middle. We all listened to the front door being opened, heavy footsteps coming down the hall, and then Warden moved away from the doorway as Talon filled it. I gulped and gripped Julian and Deanna's hands. Deanna snorted, shook off my hand, and rolled from the bed.

"That's it. You are no longer my best friend. Let it be known I am now taking interviews to fill her spot," I told the group.

She rolled her eyes at me. "Whatever."

"Oh, oh. I'll take you up on that. I want a girl bestie, and I'll stand by your side, snookums." Julian squeezed my hand. I grinned at him. Talon growled low in his throat. "O-o-or not. Later, gator." Julian moved quickly from the bed, gave me an apologetic smile, and said to Mattie, "Come on, hun, I think Thor wants alone time."

My arms went up in the air. "What the hell?" I cried, and let my arms fall back down.

The bedroom door closed. Talon stood leaning against it, watching me. I wondered if I started whistling and looking around the room, would he get the hint I wasn't ready for any type of conversation? Or it could just make him unhappier because he looked very… annoyed. Probably option two, so I refrained from whistling.

"So," I drew out.

"Tell me what your mate said wasn't true?"

"Depends on what he told you." I went for a sweet smile and raised eyebrows.

He glared. "That you'd fuckin' think I'd leave you because of what had happened to you?"

Crap.

"Uh, maybe. But really, let's look at this." I tapped my chin. "There isn't anything to leave because we aren't together."

He stiffened. I gulped and sat straighter.

"Now isn't the time for fuckin' games. I take a hike to cool my anger because I just found out my *woman,*" he clipped, "had been beaten and raped by her ex, and then some dick calls and informs me *my* woman is in her room looking scared shitless and wondering if her *man* would think she's filth." He took a step closer.

"What do I have to do to prove this is happening

between us? I want this, and I know you want this, no matter what crap you spew." He closed his eyes and took a deep breath. Upon opening them, he said, "You need me to claim your body now, is that it? If I have my dick in you, will you get that this is happening between us?" With one swoop, he removed his tee and threw it to the floor.

I tried to back up to the headboard of my bed. Waving my arms out in from of me, I perved, drooled, and yelled, "Whoa, hold up there. W-what are you doing?" *Oh, my God, I've died and gone to bad-boy heaven.*

A thought of David advancing on me like Talon was flashed through my mind.

A normal person may have been petrified in this type of situation. But I wasn't. *I* had also watched and listened to Talon for many years. I knew he talked rough, and his actions screamed scary badarse biker, but I also knew he treated women with care. No matter what he said, what he implied or had done, he would never hurt me physically or mentally.

"Proving to you that I want you. That no matter what your past was, I'd still want your hot body. You fuckin' drive me insane, kitten. I'd let no one else get away with it, do that to me. No one, kitten, but you." He was at the end of the bed now. My eyes nearly popped out of my head when he popped the button on his jeans.

My heart pounded against my chest. Every word, rude or not, *warmed* me throughout.

Still, I stuttered through my nerves, "W-wait. Holy hell—uh, wait. Put your tee on for a sec—" I covered my eyes with a hand.

"Holy shit, he's got his top off," Julian gasped from behind my bedroom door.

"Fuck, that guy moves fast," Deanna said.

"What are you two doing?" Mattie fake-whispered. The door rattled.

"I just want to see," Julian whined.

"See?" I moved my hand and pointed to the door. "We have an audience."

"Everyone better fuck off before I kill them all."

"I think he's serious," Julian said.

"We're not waiting around to find out," Mattie said.

"Fuck it," Deanna complained.

Talon knelt on the end of the bed. The sight of him, of his muscles flexing, sent a zing to the right spot.

Still, I said, "Whoa, whoa, whoa. Hold up there, slugger. I can't perform now thinking of them out there."

What was wrong with me? Why was I stopping this? *Scared.* Not of him though, of me, of falling into what he had me feeling already.

"It's fine, kitten. I'll do all the work. This time."

"Wait! What's the time?" I looked over to my alarm clock on my bedside table. "Oh, look-see, it's two. I have to pick Maya up from school soon. We'll, uh, have to get back to this another time." I nodded.

"We'll be quick." He gave me a small smile and a wink.

"No. I—uh, have a headache," I said, rubbing at my forehead.

"I'll make it better." He smirked, grabbed my ankles, and pulled me so I was flat on my back.

"Hang on. Goddamn it, Talon. Wait." I crossed my arms over my chest and glared at him as he spread my willing legs, *the hussy traitors,* and moved to kneel in between them. "I just realised I'm still shitty with you."

"You'll get over it." His hands went to each side of my waist.

"Talon. We need to talk," I said with a heavy breath as he made his way up my body until he was leaning over me. His strong arms blocked my head in, with his crotch resting against mine and my drenched panties. I closed my eyes and prayed for some resistance. It was so flipping hard! The resistance and *him.*

Yum.

I opened my eyes. God, he was gorgeous.

"You have a son?"

He closed his own eyes and cursed. "Really, you want to do this now, kitten?"

"Yep," I whispered.

No! my naughty bits screamed.

He thrust his hardness into the right spot. “Oh, hell,” I moaned and wished my clothes and his would vanish.

“Just tell me one thing before I give in to *you,*” he whispered.

“Um. Okay.” I nodded.

“You want this, between you and me?”

Shit.

“Uh...Oh.” He thrust against me again.

Damn it, clothes, be gone!

“Tell me, kitten,” he said and kissed my temple. “Tell me,” he ordered and kissed my nose.

Dear God.

“Oh, all right.” I sighed. He smiled a smile of pure satisfaction, the prick, and then rolled to my side, bringing me flush against him.

“What do you want to know about Cody?”

Okay, clothes, you can stay. “Everything,” I uttered. *Like, who in the heck is his mum, and are you still seeing her?*

“He’s a smart kid, quiet, but I think he’ll grow outta that soon. His mum and I don’t have the best relationship. We used to. We were wild together.”

A pang of jealousy hit me.

He picked up a strand of my hair and tugged it gently, then scoffed and said, “Then she turned into a bitch. She had friends and family who saw themselves as better than anyone else and eventually taught her I was scum. After Cody was born, she left; said she didn’t want him growin’ up around me and the way I lived. Funny thing though, she used to live this way as well and loved it. So now she's livin' the high, fancy fucked life with her new man."

I shouldn't have asked. To me, it sounded as though he still had feelings for her. It hurt.

Resting my hands on my stomach, I cleared my throat. "Uh, what did Cody mean last night that she was busy?"

"They had some friends over. Cody hates it. They always want him locked in his fuckin' room. I'm sure he came over just to piss her off. Can't say I blame him."

Poor Cody.

"It seemed, to me, he'd like to stay with you."

He went up onto one elbow and looked down at me. "And I'd have him, but she won't have it. I've tried. I fought her, been through the courts. They always take one fuckin' look at me and say 'hell no.'" He took my hand in his, fingers entwined.

Staring down at them for a moment, I couldn't help but notice how much I liked seeing it. I enjoyed the way his thumb ran over my own while he waited for me to speak again. What I didn't like was the smirk he had on his face when I looked up at him, because he knew I liked his hand in mine. "Um, are you still getting weekends with him?"

His smirk turned into a smile as he nodded. "Every second. This one comin'."

"Good. I'd like to get to know him."

Something flared in his eyes as he looked at me. I liked what I saw, but I couldn't trust it. He still loved his ex. The mother of his child.

"He and I would fuckin' love that. Now—" He looked over his shoulder at the clock. "We still got time to fool around, kitten."

"Uh, no."

He arched one brow. *Am I the only loser who can't do that?* "Kitten," he whispered.

"This, uh, shouldn't happen between us."

"Christ. What is going on now? You'd just said you're—"

"Wait. That wasn't me talking; that was... ah, my... um, fandola."

Both brows raised that time. "Your fuckin' what?"

"You know. My"—with my eyes, I gestured to my privates—"down there."

He smiled and then burst out laughing. "Fuck me. You can't even say pussy, vagina, cu—"

I jumped him, placing my hand over his mouth, which brought me to lie across him. His arms tightened around my waist. "No. That word is not to be used in this house." I glared.

He grinned behind my hand, his eyes turning warm.

"And anyway, we can't have anything between us when you still love your ex."

Shit, shit, shit. I shouldn't have said that. His eyes turned hard and scary. I thanked the high heavens when his phone chose that moment to ring. He sat up, and I landed back on the bed.

"What?" he hissed. "Right." He hung up and turned toward me, leaning down so our noses just touched.

Damn it, I should have taken that time to bolt for the door.

"I don't know where you got that fucked-up idea in your head, but it had better be gone when I get back."

"Um."

"No. No 'um,' I do not still love that bitch. If I did, I wouldn't be pursuing you so I could have your nice piece of arse in my bed. I don't play games, kitten. Now, kiss me."

"Huh?"

"Kiss me, kitten. I've gotta go deal with shit."

"Uh, I have to go get Maya."

"I know that. So fuckin' hurry up and kiss me and I'll see you tonight for dinner."

"What?"

"Dinner, I assume you eat it. I'll be over 'bout six."

"But Maya will be here."

"I also know that, babe. She's gotta get used to the idea of us two, may as well start tonight, and then she can meet Cody when I get him tomorrow after school."

"But—"

"Fuck it. You're takin' too long." Then he kissed me, a toe-curling, panty-dripping, tongue-bathing kiss. He pulled back and leaned his forehead against mine. "I reckon you'll be worth it. See ya tonight, kitten." And then he left.

What in the hell just happened?

CHAPTER SEVEN

I had no time to process anything. As soon as Talon left, my door swung open and in piled Deanna, Mattie, and Julian, holding a platter of crackers, cheese, and dips.

While we ate, I told them what went down.

"Oh, my fuckin' God," Deanna said when I got to the part about him coming back for tea, and Maya, and Cody, and every—freaking out—thing.

"I know, I know." I sighed and paced the room while munching on some crackers. "He thinks it's time to play family. I haven't even slept with the guy. What happens if he's no good, or he thinks I'm no good and runs a—"

"Shut the fuck up," Deanna said in her most mild-mannered way from where she sat on my bed.

I'm really starting to get sick of people telling me to shut up.

"You are both gonna rock each other's world; no doubt about that shit. And I reckon he's right. If he don't step up and get the kids involved, you'll run a fuckin' mile, scared outta your brain again."

Oh, that was low and cunning, and how come I never thought of it that way?

"I think, hun, what this chica meant when she said 'oh, my Gawd,' was regarding you thinkin' Captain America still loves his ex." Julian smiled from the bed.

"Oh."

"Yeah, oh—" Deanna began. I held up my hand.

"Before you start telling me what an idiot I am, can we leave it, 'cause I have to go get Maya?"

"You know I would have said more than idiot, but I shall delay my knocking some sense into your dumb-witted brain until later. Let's scat, people. We have a devil child to pick up."

I rolled my eyes. Maya wasn't a devil child. She was just born thirty and smarter than Deanna most times.

"Hey, where'd Vi and Warden get to anyway?" I asked as I exited my room.

"Some PI crap. Said they'd catch you sometime. Oh, and don't come in to work tomorrow since it's Friday. Start back Monday," Deanna informed me.

I turned to face her once we were in the lounge room. "That's nice of her. But I need to keep my mind occupied, and work will do that."

"I'm sure Gladiator will keep you busy enough tomorrow." Julian grinned and then looked to Mattie and back to me, saying, "Hey, nut crackers, how 'bout you two go, and we'll make a start on dinner." Julian did some weird gesture with his eyes.

It took me a second to figure out what he meant. But then it clicked: Mattie was nervous about meeting Maya for the first time.

I smiled and nodded my understanding. Actually, I was excited to bring Maya home to meet her uncle. She'd seen photos of him from when he was younger, but I didn't have any recent ones. I wondered if she would recognise him.

A pang of hurt hit me.

How was I going to explain to my six-year-old that she'd never get to meet her grandparents? I knew it would be harder for me to tell her than it would be for her to hear.

Oh, God.

Before I was allowed to wallow in worry and sorrow, Deanna pulled me toward the door and reminded me of yet another situation to worry about.

"Don't forget Zee's human vibrator will be joining us tonight."

Spotting Maya in a crowd was easier than getting Deanna not to swear. Honestly, many things were a lot easier than stopping Deanna from cussing. Maya came bounding our way with a big smile on her face and her long, dark, curly locks tied in a ponytail on top of her head.

I looked behind me at our tail. Talon had obviously asked Pick to follow us wherever we had to go. He was standing a few paces away, leaning against a car, waiting and watching. All Deanna wanted to do was go to the drug store and pick up some condoms, tampons, and pads, then call out to Pick and ask him if they were all okay. Thankfully, we didn't have time.

"Hi, Momma. Aunty Deanna. Guess what we learned today?" Maya grinned as she reached us and handed me her backpack to carry.

"Let me guess, that all boys have cooties?" Deanna asked. I smacked the back of her head.

"No-o-o."

"Your two times tables?" I asked as we made our way home with Maya skipping beside us and Pick following. I didn't understand why he wasn't just walking with us. On the way to school I tried to ask him, but before I even had a chance to take a step toward him, he barked out a 'no' and 'keep walking.'

Maya turned to me so I could see her eye roll. "Ma, I learned that in prep. You're never gonna guess, so I'll tell you. Do you know what lots of geese are called?"

"No, baby, I don't."

"A gaggle."

"Wow," Deanna said dully.

"What about asses?" Maya asked.

Deanna laughed; I hid mine with a cough. "I think you mean donkeys."

"That's what Mrs Faith said, too. But Donny said they're also called asses, and 'cause she's a teacher she can't lie, so I asked if that was true and she said yes. So do you know what a group of them are?"

"Men," Deanna muttered.

I shook my head at her and said to Maya, "No, I don't have a clue."

"A pace."

"That's interesting stuff, Maya. I'm glad you learned something today."

"Me too. So what's for dinner, Mum?"

Was every child on the face of the planet programmed to ask that question after school? I think they were.

"Not sure just yet. But I have a surprise for you," I said as we walked up the front steps to the porch.

"Oh, what, what?"

I opened the front door. There was some noise coming from the kitchen, and then Mattie and Julian came running around the corner, excitement, and concern in their eyes.

I gave Maya time to dissect the newcomers. She looked from one to the other, and then at me with a smile upon her sweet face.

"That's my uncle, right?" She pointed to Mattie, who was grinning from ear to ear. Julian's hand went to his mouth, tears welling in his eyes.

"Yes, sweetie. That's my brother, Mattie, your uncle. And with him is Julian, Mattie's partner."

Mattie's shocked eyes rose to mine. He was worried about me telling Maya he was gay, but I already knew it wouldn't faze her.

"Cool," she said, and walked over to Mattie. He bent to hug her, but she reached out first and placed her hand upon his cheek. "You got Mum's eyes. That's how I knew." Her smile grew. "Hi, Uncle Mattie." She wrapped her arms around his neck and hugged him tightly.

I pulled my lips into a tight line to hold back my own emotions.

"Well, ain't this ducking grand," Deanna said beside me. "I hate emotional sh...stuff." I watched her wipe away a tear and laughed. "Flock off, you." She glared at me.

We both looked back to Maya as she stood in front of Julian. "Can I call you my uncle, too?"

Julian looked at the ceiling and back down at Maya. "Oh, sweet honey dew, of course you can." They hugged.

I WAS LEANING against the kitchen bench, watching Julian and Deanna sitting at the table arguing about some answers for Maya's homework. Maya sat with them, doing a good job of ignoring them both and continuing her way through it. Not that there was a lot anyway; some reading and spelling words. She was only six, for goodness' sake. Mattie was busy next to me, finishing off the casserole for tea that he'd prepared earlier.

Seeing this made me feel happy, yet sad. I loved to watch people; I was a watcher from way back, and what I was seeing was that I finally had a house full of family that I loved.

Only I was never going to see my parents again, and that hurt.

A hand fell on top of mine on the bench. I looked down; it was Mattie's, and I glanced up to his sad eyes, and I knew he knew what I had been thinking. It was his way of showing me things would be okay.

I could only hope.

"All right, people, clear the table," Mattie called. "And don't worry, Maya honey, I'll help you later, so you'll have all the right answers." He grinned. Maya sighed in relief and nodded at her uncle.

"School sucks anyway, kiddo," Deanna said. "You should just quit, become an actress, and support your mum and me for the rest of our lives."

"Deanna," I warned.

"Don't listen to her, sugar plum. School is great. Learning is better, so then you can get a high-paying job and *then* support us all." Julian winked at Maya, who giggled in return. I rolled my eyes and thanked the high heaven that Maya knew they were talking nonsense.

The table had been cleared of schoolwork when the front door opened, and I froze with knives and forks in my hands. All of us turned to the kitchen doorway to see Talon in his godly form walk in.

"Talon!" Maya chirped.

While my woman bits chirped for him.

Maya ran at him. He lifted her up and twirled her around. Not something you'd see a hard-core biker do every day.

"Maya, you been good today?" he asked after he placed her feet back on the floor.

"I'm always good, Talon. Whatcha doin' here?"

Talon raised his eyes to me, questioning me in his silent way on what I'd told her. I chose to glance at a spot on the kitchen ceiling and bite my bottom lip.

Is that a growl coming from him? Shit.

"I came to have a word with your momma. Could you give us a minute?" We all knew that wasn't a question. He stalked over to me, grabbed the knives and forks out of my hands, placed them behind me, then took my wrist and pulled me from the room, down the hall, and into my bedroom.

Before he closed my door, we heard Maya squeal and announce to the people in the kitchen, "I hope he's going to kiss her. They're always lookin' at each other with yucky love eyes." They burst out laughing. Talon closed the door and faced me with a smirk.

"Talon—"

"No, kitten, even your daughter can see something has been going on between us for a while now. All I want to know is what you're going to tell her?"

I waved my hands up and down, my eyes bugging out of my head—not a pretty look. "What am I supposed to tell her?"

"That you're my woman and I'm your man. That she'll be seein' a lot more of me around 'ere."

I sat on the edge of the bed and looked at the floor. This was it. I was going to have to be honest. "It's not that simple, Talon. I'm not one of your bimbos who you can screw over. I need stability for Maya and me. I need long term—"

"Seriously, Zara," he clipped. "If I thought you were just some bimbo to warm my fuckin' dick for the night, I wouldn't be here. Hell," he rumbled. In the next second, he was on his knees in front of me. With one finger under my chin, he raised my head. Our eyes met, and my heart skipped a beat.

I was about to have a heart attack.

I watched him lick his lips, and then those lips turned into a smirk because he knew I was watching them.

"I hate this talkin' shit. I want you as my woman.

Long-fuckin'-term. I know we still got a lotta shit we need to learn 'bout one another, but that's the best part. For once in my life, I'll try to be patient, for you."

Oh, my flipping God.

Was Talon worth risking my heart being broken?

Especially now?

Did I trust him?

Shit. Heck. Dick—yes, Talon's.

"Okay," I whispered.

His eyes flared. He let out a breath, and he smiled a burn-your-eyes-out-'cause-it-was-so-hot smile. One I had never seen before on his lickable mouth.

Then, thank the high heavens, his mouth was on mine, demanding and sensual. I was all too willing to comply with whatever his needs were. My hands curled into his hair, pulling him closer; his groan of approval made me smile. One of his hands traced from my hip up to my breast.

Shit, did he just press a magic nipple button to send a wave of lust down to my core?

Yep. I had magic nipples.

Holy Moses, that feels great.

Talon brought up his other hand to cradle the side of my face, and I wrapped my legs around his waist and moaned when I felt his large-oh-crap-will-it-fit penis rub against my centre.

A knock on the door broke through my horny fog.

"Uh, guys," Mattie whispered. "Can you hold off on the sex right now? Tea's ready and we're hungry."

Talon leaned his forehead against mine and muttered some curse words. Then he said, "One fuckin' time we'll get to finish this. And honestly, I don't want people around, because if your pussy is as demanding as your mouth, I won't want to leave, or anyone to interrupt."

With that, he got up, adjusted himself, and walked out the door.

I could not believe he just said that. I did not have a demanding... fandola.

"Talon!" I yelled.

He stalked back to the room, grinned, kissed me hard, grabbed my hand, and started for the kitchen once again. Only this time, he was dragging me behind him.

We walked into the kitchen. Everyone was already seated around the small table. Two places were left, one for me and one for the Neanderthal. I watched Maya's eyes go from our faces to our joined hands, and then she smiled.

"Are you stayin' for dinner, Talon? My uncle made it." I could hear the pride in her voice.

"Yeah, I'm staying," Talon said, and sat down next to me at the table.

Somehow, when he said 'I'm staying', I was sure he meant more than just for tea.

CHAPTER EIGHT

Concentrating at dinner was hard. Talon sat next to me; sometimes he would rest one hand on the back of my chair, and other times he would play with the ends of my hair. All of it made my brain go ga-ga. Still, the conversation went on, and by the time we'd all finished, I felt full and content.

I turned to Maya. "I'm just going to help clean up, and then we'll do your reader before bed." I rose and took some plates to the sink.

Talon came up behind me, and with an arm around my waist, he whispered, "Can I help Maya with her reader?"

I went stiff and closed my eyes.

It had always been just me.

"Kitten," he uttered, "that mean somethin' to you?"

I nodded.

"Good." He kissed my cheek and turned to Maya. "Come on, squirt, you're readin' to me tonight."

"Yay," she sang, and bounced up and out to her room with Talon following.

I turned around from the sink and my eyes met Deanna's. She also knew it meant something *big* to me.

With a hushed voice, she said, "Well, thank fuck—"

"Deanna. Language," I snapped.

"Oh, give me a break. I can only go so long, and she can't hear me now." She grabbed the rest of the plates and brought them to the bench. "It's good to see, Zee. It's so good to see."

"I double that," Julian said from the table, where he sat next to a smiling Mattie. "I haven't known you long, sponge cake, but you deserve this. Him."

"He's right, Zee," Mattie added. "I can see you're scared, but let it happen. I think with Talon beside you, you'll both shine for that precious girl in there." He pointed in the direction of Maya's room.

I pulled my lips between my teeth and nodded.

"No need to be holding out anymore, bitch. What you have right there in that room is fuckin' worth holding on to," Deanna said. "Right, enough said. Let's get this shit cleaned and go veg out before I gotta hit the road."

That was yet another worry I had to voice. "I don't want you going home alone, Deanna."

"I don't want to hear this. I'm fine; I reckon you're worrying over nothing. And besides, it's not like he'd come after me. Hell, he doesn't know who I am."

"You don't know that. He could be watching. I think from now on you should move in here."

She rolled her eyes and became a little rougher with the dishes as she loaded them in the dishwasher.

"If you break even one plate, I'll have to hurt you. And don't go ignoring me, wench."

"I love the relationship they have," Julian said to Mattie.

"It's a little strange," Mattie added.

"But strange is beautiful." Julian smiled.

"Whatever, meat slappers." Deanna rolled her eyes. "Look, it's going to be fine. I'm going home, and that's the end of the story."

"No, you're not." We all looked at the doorway to see Griz standing there glaring at Deanna.

"Did anyone hear him come in?" I asked. They shook their heads. "Great lot we'd be if we were ninja attacked."

I watched Deanna face Griz with her hands on her hips, head held high. With her upper lip raised, she snapped, "Yes. I. Fuckin'. Am."

"You do all this tough-talking, and telling Wildcat there to keep herself safe by staying and trusting. Why don't you do the same?"

"Yeah!" I yelled and fist-pumped the air.

Deanna snarled at me to shut up, and then said to Griz, “Because he won’t be after me, oh wise one.” She raised one eyebrow.

“You can’t be sure of that. If he’s watching Wildcat, then he’ll do anything to get at her; meaning, he won’t have a second thought of taking out someone she cares about.”

I gasped. “What about Maya at school? I’ll have to keep her home.”

“No, darlin’, she’s covered by the boys. Someone will always be there watchin’, so you don’t need to stress.”

I nodded, though I still felt uneasy.

Griz turned a hard stare on Deanna. “You’ll be staying at the compound. In my room.”

She smirked and crossed her arms over her chest. “Well, hot stuff, if all you wanted was to get me into bed, all you had to was ask.”

He straightened. “You’ll be in my bed, on your own. You ain’t my type, princess—too young and just a pain in the arse.”

“Yeah, right, handsome, I bet every morning when you’re in the shower you jerk your chain thinkin’ of this arse.” She slapped her butt.

Griz growled.

Julian giggled. “Did she honestly just say that?”

I sighed.

Mattie nodded while looking concerned.

"Jesus Christ." Griz shook his head. I thought he would have put her down or stalked off, but instead, he said, "That's right, sweetheart. I come every morning thinking of bangin' you so hard it'd work some of that pole outta your arse. As I'm sure you fiddle with your nub every day thinking of how hard and long I'd take you."

"Oh, boy, is it getting hot in here?" Julian asked, fanning himself.

I looked back at Deanna, surprised she was still silent and shocked to see a blush upon her cheeks.

"Fuck you," Deanna uttered.

He smirked. He knew he'd just won. "In your dreams, princess. Now, Pick will meet you out front when you're finished here. He'll show you to your room. You better not fuckin' fight him on this," he said, and then walked out of the house.

"Deanna?" I pressed.

"Shut the fuck up. I don't wanna hear it."

"He's a nice guy," I said.

She snorted. "Too old for me. What is he, fifty?"

"Forty," Talon said as he came into the room, up to me, and moved my body so he could stand behind me with his arms around my waist.

Holy heck did that feel special. It had been so long since I felt something for someone. I forgot all about the heart palpitations, the butterflies, and weak knees. I wanted to cherish it for a little longer, just standing there in his arms. However, I needed to change the subject before Deanna had a full-blown hissy fit, so I said, "Come on y'all, I need a Jensen Ackles fix. *Supernatural* is on soon."

Any woman who didn't find Jensen strip-worthy was insane in my books.

Deanna smiled at me. She knew I was taking the attention away from her and she appreciated it. Didn't mean I wouldn't drill her later on what all the sexual tension was with her and Griz. Not many men would go head-to-head with Deanna, and I think she'd finally met her match. I wanted to jump with glee.

Julian groaned. "Honey, I'll watch *Supernatural* and get freaked the fuck out, but only if you all watch *Burlesque* with me. I brought it from home."

We all moved from the kitchen to the lounge and found seats.

"Oh, I am so there. But we all gotta go say goodnight to Maya first."

Maya was more than happy to have everyone in her room showering her with hugs and kisses. We then all filed out to the living room. I sat between Deanna and Talon on the couch. Actually, I was more on Talon's side, leaning against his chest because he'd hooked an arm around my shoulders and pulled me against him.

To start off with, I'd been stiff; of course, I got over it when his luscious voice whispered in my ear to relax.

Mattie and Julian squeezed themselves into the lounge chair together, moaning about how fake *Supernatural* was; not that it stopped Julian from squealing and hiding his eyes with Mattie's hand on the more scary parts. Once *Supernatural* finished—pout—we started *Burlesque.* Another favourite on my movie list.

"You know, I'd turn gay for Christina Aguilera," I announced. I felt Talon chuckle beside me.

"Not if I got to her first." Deanna yawned.

I shoved her and said, "Dude, she'd have my shoes under her bed way before your stinky ones."

"Actually, I'd have to agree; she is hot. I think I'd even turn straight for her," Mattie said, receiving a look from Julian. We laughed.

It was a great movie. I had to rewind it three times to the part where she sang on stage for the first time. Just as it was finishing up there was a knock on the door; we all looked at each other while Talon stood and walked over to answer it.

"Boss," Pick said with a chin lift. His deep blue eyes looked stressed. He ran a hand over his buzz cut, and then scratched his cute goatee.

"S'up?" Talon asked.

Pick looked over Talon's shoulder; his gaze fell upon Deanna, and then went back to Talon. "Griz said to come grab her if I had to take off anywhere. I have to take off, boss."

"What's happenin'? I thought Griz was 'round tonight; he could have come himself."

"He thought so too." Pick leaned in closer. "She called."

Huh, what? Say again, or just speak the frig up. Who's she?

I glanced at Deanna and knew from her drawn brows she was wondering the same thing.

"Again? Fuck," Talon barked. "Where you gotta go?"

"Need to help my ma with somethin'. Griz didn't want to leave it to the recruits. The others are busy either workin', drinkin', or fuckin'. So I gotta take her over and lock her down before I leave."

Talon nodded. He turned to the room. "Hell Mouth, time to get your arse outta here."

"Does it bother anyone how bossy these pricks are?" Deanna asked the room.

"Yeah, a little bit," I answered because sometimes it was also downright *hot*.

"You know I can walk across the road on my own. I ain't no fuckin' child."

Pick sighed. "I was told if you pulled any shit, I was to haul you over there over my shoulder. Is that how you want it, woman?"

Deanna got up, grumbling and no doubt cursing under her breath the whole way to the front door. "See you losers tomorrow." She waved over her shoulder and Talon closed the door.

"Well," Mattie yawned, "I'm buggered. I'm going to hit the hay."

"I'll join you, honey," Julian said. "Leave these two love birds alone." Julian added a wink.

Why did I all of a sudden feel very nervous?

"Wait." I bounced up from the couch. "Ah, doesn't anyone want a hot chocolate? A coffee? A shot of something stronger?" *I know I could use one.*

"No thanks, sis," Mattie said. He and Julian both came over and kissed me on the cheek goodnight. And no matter how much I pleaded with my eyes, the dicks went off to their room.

I faced Talon. "Well, I guess it's time for bed."

He gave me a chin lift. "Right, I'll lock up."

That was easy. "Okay. I'll, ah, see you. Thanks, you know. Ah, night." Maybe I should have given him a kiss goodnight, but I was a chicken and bolted for my room while Talon locked up and went home.

I got ready for bed while pondering how easy it had been getting rid of Talon. I thought he would have grabbed me or said something like 'Kitten, what the fuck are you forgettin'?'

I slid under the covers and it dawned on me. I kind of had hoped he would've said or done something, and now

I was disappointed that he hadn't made an effort. Maybe he was getting sick of me already?

My bedroom door opened and Talon walked in. I couldn't keep the smile off my face.

"You thought I was goin'," Talon said with a chuckle. "I am damn happy to see that smile on ya face from just knowing I'm still here." He pulled his tee off in one quick swoop.

The smile fell from my face and I sat up. "You, ah, can't stay here."

He sighed loudly. "And why the hell not?" he asked while removing his jeans, leaving him in black boxers.

Hallelujah! My magic nipples and fandola sang.

"Um, because of Maya."

"Jesus, kitten. I'm stayin'. Look, if it'll make you feel better, I'll move to the couch before she wakes up. But right now, I wanna sleep with my woman in my arms." He walked to the side of the bed, lifted the covers, which I was clinging to, and climbed in.

What could I say? He was willing to move to the couch so I wouldn't worry if Maya thought we were moving too fast.

Or was it that I thought we were moving too fast?

I didn't know; my brain felt scrambled. I still had so many things to worry about. Was David out there watching me? When was he going to strike? Was I just overreacting with…well, everything?

"You gonna sit up all night, babe?" he asked, his deep voice sending a shiver down my spine.

God, even my spine is happy he's here.

I looked over my shoulder. He had one arm behind his head and the other was outstretched for me to lie upon. My heart was already going wild, but it stepped up to an even more frenzied rhythm. And why did it sound like it was pumping to the beat of "Bad to the Bone"?

"Damn, kitten. Are you always this nervous?" He chuckled.

"No." I glared. "Only around you." *And when psychopaths are looking for me.*

"Good to know." He smiled and pulled me down so my head rested on his chest and his arm held me tightly around my waist. He kissed the top of my head and uttered again, "Good to know."

"Talon?"

"Yeah, babe?"

"Can I ask you something?"

"Only if it's quick. 'Cause the more you talk whispery, the more my dick gets hard, and I can't fuck ya with a house full."

I smiled. It was good to know I affected him like he did on me. I rolled into him more and bravely slid my hand from his stomach to his chest. His hand came down upon mine.

"Kitten, you keep being cute-like, I'm gonna have to

take you. I've only got so much fuckin' restraint. Ask your question and let's get some shut-eye."

"Well." I cleared my throat and had to think real hard what my question was again because all that was on my mind was Talon taking me. "Um, I was wondering why you and Violet aren't close."

He started to trace circles on my hip. I wanted to purr.

"She didn't want me to get involved in our uncle's club. He came to us eight years ago and said he wanted to give me the chance to run Hawks if anything happened to him. I felt honoured. Violet felt disgusted. We both knew the club was running drugs and selling women." I couldn't help but stiffen. Talon felt it, but he continued, "Vi thought it'd lead me down the wrong path. It did for a while, and Vi hated that; in turn, she hated me, because by then she was on the other side of the law. I lost her trust, I lost her love, and her in total as a sister. Then my uncle passed away five years ago. I was in charge and encouraged my brothers to run a clean club. The club members look after each other; we own three Harley stores over Victoria and have a few strip clubs. Look, we no longer do any of that past shit, but it doesn't mean we don't help out. An ex-member left 'cause he still wanted to deal with hookers. Outta respect, we look out for his woman while they're on our territory. Babe, there's a lotta dicks out there who don't believe the club's clean, but I don't give a fuck. I'm happy, and my brothers are happy."

"So, ah, across the road is... um, just the compound?"

"Yeah. But at the side is a mechanical business and it's also where I manage *all* club businesses from. Never fuckin' thought I'd spend most of my life on a phone or computer doin' that kinda shit. The only good part about it is that I've got many members to fall back on when I don't want'a deal with the crap. That's when I get to take off on my Harley, whenever I fuckin' please."

"Okay." I nodded. "So, nothing untoward happens over there? Like... um, those friends and their hookers rocking up?"

"Babe, none of us have to pay for pussy. And yeah, we fuckin' party hard, but that's it. My life is clean, kitten. If it wasn't, I wouldn't have involved you in it." With one quick movement, he was on top of me, studying my face for something. "You're too good for that kinda shit."

I blushed and nodded, my arms encircling his waist. "Do—" I stopped when he spread my legs with his knees. "Uh, do... do you think that you and Vi could make up?"

He kissed my neck. "Maybe one day," he said, and then his eyes met mine. "You surprise me, kitten. I like that about you. I tell you I was involved in shit and you take it in stride, thinking nothing of it."

I smiled at him. "Everyone has had shit in their lives, Talon. What makes a person is if they can climb out of it before it hurts more people, and I believe you have. You've also succeeded at it."

He closed his eyes and rested his forehead against mine. "I gotta have a bit of you, babe. I can't fuckin' wait. You gotta be quiet, kitten. All right?"

Shit a doodle duck. Was I all right with him 'having a bit of me?' What did he *mean* by a bit of me? I didn't know, but my body did because my head nodded without my brain's acknowledgment.

CHAPTER NINE

Talon grinned wickedly at me. He kissed me hard, but all too soon his lips left mine. I was about to complain when I felt them at my neck. I arched to give him better access. Licks, bites, and kisses he delivered upon my neck, and then slowly he moved to my collarbone. I let out a moan. He shushed me, but I felt his grin on my skin.

I was feeling overwhelmed like I was being touched for the first time. Maybe I had become a born-again virgin.

As his lips played, his hands roamed from my hips up under my t-shirt to my magic nipples and ultra-sensitive breasts. He tugged my tee up further; my slutty arms rose on their own and he threw my t-shirt to the floor.

Finally, he moved lower. I had been just about ready

to strum my fingers on the bed while waiting for his mouth to be on my breasts. Now I didn't have to. Only he wasn't there long enough. He went to move on, but I wasn't ready for that yet; I pulled him by his hair and positioned his mouth back where I wanted it. He chuckled and bit down on my magic nipple, causing a moan to escape.

"Quiet, kitten," he growled.

"Seriously?" How was that even possible with a lover like him? I glared down at him as he stared back with his teeth clamped around my nipple. He bit. I shoved my fist in my mouth, smothering my moan.

Jesus, if he doesn't get a move on, I'm going to combust.

"Talon. Honey. If you don't get a move on, I'll come on my own."

He stopped his attention to my stomach and hips and looked up, smiling. "So eager."

"Well, when it's been six years—"

I didn't get to finish what I was going to rant about. He hissed, my shorts and underwear disappeared, and his mouth was feasting upon the most vital—right now, anyway—part of my body.

The shock of the invasion caused me to cry out. It wasn't long before his lips and tongue brought me to a climax.

"Fuck. You taste un-fuckin'-real."

Oh. My. God. I was mortified that I'd lasted seconds. I

covered my eyes with my arm; I knew my face was burning bright red. Talon settled between my legs; his arms folded across my hips and I knew his head was rested on those arms, watching and waiting for me while my body and breath recovered, along with my dignity.

"Kitten," Talon said.

Holy shit. Did my stomach just wobble when he spoke? That was beyond mortifying. I wanted to die. He was so used to perfection, and yet here he had a woman who hadn't had sex in… forever, and only took a second to climax, while he stared at my cellulite.

I felt the bed shift. Talon climbed up my body and lay next to me, his arousal at my hip. He tugged my arm.

"No," I stated. "You, ah, better go to the couch now." *Wait*. That was kind of rude of me. No one had gone *down there* before, so shouldn't I be showing my appreciation? Maybe if I did I wouldn't be so embarrassed; he could have something wrong with him. Then we'd be even.

I was going to have to do this fast, so he didn't see my wobbly bits doing their own jig.

I pounced. My arm flew out, knocking him in the head. He swore; I mumbled a sorry as I spread his legs with my hands while he was in a daze. Before he got a good look at me moving, I rested between his legs with the sheet over me. I grabbed the waist of his boxers and pulled down; his erection sprang free.

Talon's hands lay over mine, stopping me. That was

okay because I was still in shock from seeing a cock. *Gulp, so freaking big.* Or was it just the average size? From the experience I'd had in the past, I wasn't sure. But there was the possibility that if Talon and I had a chance to do the dirty, he would be impaling me on his hard pole.

"I like the way you're looking at me, kitten. And I love the fact that you just licked your lips. But why in the fuck did you pull a speed marathon to get down there? I didn't eat you just to have you return the favour."

"Um," I said to his perfect pecker. Damn him. Why did he look so fucking good? *The prick.* "It's not about returning the favour. I want to do this." His cock twitched with…glee? I realised then that it was true. I wanted to please him, and that thought also pleasured me.

Before he could say any more, I went deep. My whole mouth covered all of him, making my eyes water. *Huge.* I pulled up slowly and flicked my tongue side-to-side along the way.

"Fuck," Talon hissed, arching and fisting the sheets.

I loved seeing that reaction from him. That it was me causing him to do that. I swirled my tongue at the tip and gently bit. Talon growled. I smiled and went down once again, taking my sweet time.

"Kitten," he warned. He wanted faster; I wanted to go slower and memorise the way his body moved, the way his eyes closed when I reach the base of his cock, and started back up once again.

He fisted my hair tightly; I moaned. Our eyes met; desire pooled in both. With the pressure of his hand in my hair, Talon took control; his cock slid in and out of my mouth perfectly. I clenched my legs together; what I wanted was to let my fingers do their job and finish me off once again. My body was craving to be pumped like my mouth was. It was such a friggin' turn-on. Something I had never felt before and wanted to feel for the rest of my life.

"Hell, kitten." Talon closed his eyes and moaned. He was close; I could taste it.

He let go of my hair. I kept the pace going on my own, enjoying the rush of seeing him spread out and exposed.

"Fuck, I'm gonna come, babe," he groaned.

His first shot reached the back of my throat; I drank it down with the rest. Even after there was no more, I tightened my grip at the base and pulled up, squeezing the last drop out before licking it off.

I was about to wrap the sheet around me, but before I could, hands came under my arms, and I was pulled up to lie across Talon's naked body. My legs went around his waist, my arms to each side of him; I looked down, my hair spilling around my shoulders. I was shocked and happy to see that my own naked body wasn't making it hard for him to breathe.

He grinned up at me. "No one has ever sucked me that hard or taken it to the very last drop. That was fuckin' heaven, kitten."

A blush filled my cheeks, and I looked away. *Now I blush, what the hell?*

He laughed. "No need to go shy on me now, babe." He pulled me down and kissed me stupid. His expert mouth moved to my ear and he whisper-growled, "Don't ever fuckin' hide your body from me again. I love every inch; and eventually, I will have tasted every inch, going back for more and more until I die."

Oh. My. Fucking. God. Words like that were going to make it hard for me to not fall for this biker.

"Let's get some sleep before I have to fuckin' move." He rolled me to his side and tucked me close. One of his arms went around my shoulders as I rested my head on his chest. His other hand took one of mine and placed them on his stomach. I entwined one leg through his.

Again, he had me feeling safe, warm, and protected, even cared for. I wanted to cry.

WAKING up feeling well rested was something out of the ordinary for me. I stretched as moments of last night played on repeat in my mind. I smiled and reached out to the side Talon occupied last night. He wasn't there. I giggled; he had moved after all. I had been so sedated I didn't feel him leave.

My bedroom door opened. I pulled the sheet around me tightly as Maya skipped into the bedroom and onto the bed.

"Morning, sweetheart," I said as she plopped down next to me.

"Mornin', Momma. I had a dream last night. Wanna know what it was about?"

"Sure." I rolled to my side and faced her as she looked up at the ceiling.

"Toby, from school, was being mean to Becka, so I kicked him in the balls."

I closed my eyes, only to open them when the room filled with deep laughter. Talon was standing in the doorway.

"That's good, kid. Even in your dreams, you gotta protect the ones you care for."

I rolled my eyes. Still, I couldn't help but smile at Talon. "But you have to remember that kicking a boy there can hurt them a lot."

"I know, Momma. So I'll only do it when they really annoy me."

Talon chuckled again. "Come on, kiddo. I'll make you breakfast; let your ma get up and ready."

She grinned and bounced down to the end of the bed, then stopped. She looked from Talon to me. "Momma?"

"Yes, baby?"

"Talon's your boyfriend now, right?"

I froze. That I wasn't expecting, so early in the freaking morning. What could I say though, after what happened last night? I looked up to Talon; he stared back with a worried expression. "Yes, Maya. He is my boyfriend."

"More than that, kitten." He smirked and turned to Maya to say, "I'm her man, baby girl."

"Cool." She beamed, and then her face was puzzled. "Then how come Talon was sleeping on the couch when I came out this mornin'? Shouldn't he be in here with you?"

Talon chuckled. I blanched.

"From now on, Maya, that's where I'll be," Talon said.

She shrugged and said, "Okay." Then bolted out of the room with Talon chuckling and following behind her.

I flopped to my back, placed the pillow Talon had used over my face and screamed. How was it possible that children were so carefree when it came to life-changing situations? Ones that would freak any adult out? Just like it had me when anything regarding Talon and me happened.

I was prepared to lie there for quite some time and debate on what to do next. Should I panic some more over the fact that my daughter wasn't fazed by the fact that I would now be having a man sleep in my bed? A bed that she jumped into nearly every morning to wake my zombie form up from? Or should I leave things as they were, and not bother freaking out about anything that just occurred?

All thoughts soon left me, because Talon's scent from the pillow distracted me, sending image after image of last night into my mind.

It was time for me to get up and have a cold shower.

I walked into the kitchen wearing a long, striped black-and-grey skirt with a black tee that read 'Get Low and Go'. My hair was still wet from the shower, so I left it down. No doubt, by midmorning I would have to put it up because it would turn out to be one big frizz bomb since I'd run out of my hair product that kept the curl at bay.

I snorted. Let's see how Talon handled that look; he could still run a mile.

Rounding the corner, I stopped dead. Maya was sitting at the table in her school uniform. Yeah, that was fine. Mattie and Julian were leaning against each other and the bench. Yeah, that was fine also. What had me going *o-kay* and made my eyes pop from my head was Talon, my badarse biker man, standing behind Maya and doing her hair in a ponytail, with a flipping ribbon to boot.

Talon's hard eyes turned to me. "Do not say a freakin' word," he growled.

My heart swelled. I wanted to run to him and maul him like a wild woman. Not only was he caring for me by caring for my daughter, but he was doing it in front of witnesses. To top it off, he actually listened to me and chose not to swear in front of Maya.

Shit. Tears were forming in my eyes.

Talon's eyes stayed on me as I saw them turn sweet. He knew it meant something to me, and just in case he didn't, I walked over to him and gently kissed him. My lips met his, and when I went to pull away, he pinned me back with his hand around my waist and deepened the kiss.

"Aw, yuck," Maya moaned.

I smiled against Talon's mouth. He chuckled. I stepped out of his reach and went to the coffee machine on the counter. Though I didn't miss the gentle shove Talon gave Maya, or the wide happy smile that was on her lips.

If this was how it was going to be, I could handle that.

"Mornin', guys," I said to the two grinning fools. I hipped Mattie out of the way of me reaching my morning coffee. "Get outta my way. If I don't have my fix in the next twenty seconds, all heck will break loose, and it's way worse than me PMSing." I took a sip and turned to Talon. "Let that be a warning to you."

"Got that, kitten." He smirked.

A knock sounded on the front door.

"Open up, duck heads, I *need* a good coffee," Deanna yelled. Mattie moved off to the front door.

"Momma, can I go play before school?"

"Have you had breakfast?"

"Yeah, Talon got it for me."

Wipe the tears off my heart.

"Teeth?"

She rolled her eyes. "Yes, Momma, Talon already told me to."

Forget wiping tears, let the flood begin.

"And I can see Talon has already done your hair. So yes, baby, you can play. We'll leave in ten."

"Okay." She got up from the table and ran out of the room, calling a quick hello to Deanna on the way past.

"Coffee, bitch, quick," Deanna ordered.

I got a cup ready and handed it to her as she sat down at the table. Talon walked over to me and placed me in front of him, his arms around my waist. It seemed to be his usual stance when I was concerned. Not that I minded at all. I sighed and relaxed into him. He grunted his approval of me not fighting him on the close comfort he was offering after taking care of my young. *And melting my heart into a big puddle of goo. The hairy ball sac.* Though, I couldn't help the smile creeping onto my lips.

"Yo, boss man," Deanna started after her first sip. "You gotta get better fuckin' coffee at the compound. It nearly choked the hell outta me." She shuddered from the memory.

"You got work today?" I asked Deanna.

"Yeah." She rolled her eyes.

"Who in their right mind hired someone with such a colourful vocabulary?" Julian asked. Mattie nodded in agreement as he leaned back in his seat and placed an arm around Julian's chair.

I giggled. "The library."

Talon chuckled behind me. "You have got to be shittin' me."

Deanna flipped him the middle finger and then swung it to Julian.

"Oh, don't give me that, caramel cake. I think it's a great job for you. All that silence." He snickered. "No wonder you swear like a trooper when you've been cooped up all day."

I cleared my throat. "Actually, she only works a thirteen-hour week."

Julian raised his eyebrows and turned to Deanna. "I guess all the colourfulness just comes naturally."

Deanna snorted. "That's right, sugarplum. Anyway, now that I've had my fill of all your shit, people, I better be off." She rose from the table, bringing her mug to the sink.

"Who's on you today?" Talon asked.

Huh? What does he mean?

Deanna sighed loudly. "I don't need no arsewipe babysitter."

Well, that explained that.

Talon's phone rang, and he answered with a gruff, "What? Yep, she is. That right. Okay." He flipped the phone closed and placed it back in his pocket. "Don't fuckin' move a muscle," he ordered.

I moved out of his arms and faced him with a glare. "Don't you talk to me like that; and I'm not moving, and keep down the tone. Maya's still in the house."

He smirked. "I wasn't talkin' to you, kitten." He nodded over my shoulder. I turned to see Deanna near the doorway, looking out into the lounge with a tense body.

"Deanna?" I asked.

Julian squealed. "Whoo-boy, something's going to go down. I so love this place. It's like having your own private movie. Wait, I need a snack while watching this."

"You just had breakfast," Mattie said, shaking his head.

"Come on—"

"Guys," I interrupted, and then spun back to Talon. "What's wrong?"

"That was Griz on the phone; he asked Hell Mouth to wait while he had a quick shower. He got out, and she'd disappeared."

Deanna turned back around, hands on her hips and a

scowl on her face. “Oh, come the fuck on. I needed a coffee.”

“You could have waited.” Talon glared back at her. “Have some fuckin’ respect, woman. Griz had a shit night; he doesn’t wanna deal with your crap all day, but he is.”

“Whatever.” She shook her head and looked at me. “This is what you call friendship. Now I have to put up with a body-fuckin’-guard all day and night.”

I gasped. She was right; I was a terrible friend. All my past poo now affected her life in more ways than she could handle. I know Deanna; she’d hate being crowded all the time.

“Don’t start all your wah-wah crap.” She rolled her eyes and walked over to me. Our gazes met. “You know I wouldn’t have it any other way. I love ya guts.”

I nodded. She smiled, and the front door banged open.

“Get your arse out here, woman, or you’ll be late for work,” Griz snarled.

“I’m coming!” Deanna yelled back. She sighed, hugged me, and made her way out. “See you losers later.”

CHAPTER TEN

Talon and I walked Maya to school. We walked Maya—my daughter—to school. As in together. Both of us walking with Maya, to school. Like a real-life couple. It felt amazing. He held my hand. Maya held his other hand, and as we walked, we talked. More like Maya talked to Talon, and I walked along while trying not to bawl my eyes out, trip, or sing, "The hills are alive with the sound of music."

Once we got back to my place, he announced, "Kitten, I gotta take off for a while. Blue's coming over, but I'll be back later before you hav'ta get Maya from school. I'm gonna bring some of my shit with me to keep here; saves me travelling home every day."

I gulped. This was serious stuff. Still, I couldn't stop

from saying, "Talon, you live right next door. It's not that hard."

He laughed. "Babe, I don't live there. I sometimes crash there when I've had too much. I live out on some land in Buninyong." He kissed me before I had a chance to think.

I went to my tippy toes and tightly wrapped my arms around his neck. He growled deeply, sending a shiver to my fandola. I loved it when he did that. Our tongues did the tango with the expertise of practiced partners.

"Ah, don't mind us."

I moved my head back enough to look over Talon's shoulder, panting, and saw Julian and Mattie standing in the kitchen doorway. I wanted to hiss and yell at them to flock off. But I was also grateful they turned up, or I'd be turning myself inside out to claw my way into Talon's pants.

"Fuck it. One day, kitten, one day, I'll have you, and then you won't be glad to be interrupted."

I looked into his amused crinkled eyes. "Well, I wasn't totally happy about it."

"I agree," Julian said. "She was giving us laser eyes."

"That's good to know." He smiled down at me, kissed my forehead, and moved off to the front door. "I'll pick up some takeout for dinner after I get Cody from his mother," he said over his shoulder.

"No need, Thor. Mattie and I are going shopping; we'll have enough to feed an army."

I raised my hand to get his attention. "Oh, um, what's Cody's favourite meal to eat?"

Talon's warm eyes turned to me. "Any kinda roast, kitten, just like his dad."

I looked over to Mattie and said, "Can you get me a leg of lamb?"

"Sure thing." He smiled.

"He'll love it, babe," Talon said. "I'll catch ya later."

Five seconds after Talon left, Blue walked in. Maybe I should lock that door one day, but now it seemed to be the traffic way for hot bikers.

"Hey, baby." Blue grinned and walked—no, more like stalked—over to me, and ran the back of his hand down the side of my cheek. My eyes widened as he nodded over my shoulder to Julian and Mattie.

"Alrighty, we're off down the street, hun," Julian said. "If you think of anything else, text me, *baby*." He wiggled his eyebrows up and down. Then he coughed under his breath, "Slut."

I gave him an eye roll. "Uh, wait. Um…" I turned to Blue. "Shouldn't we walk with them, to keep them covered?"

"Everything is set, baby. As soon as someone steps out of this house, another is upon them."

Wow. Talon wasn't taking any chances.

"We're going in Julian's car," Mattie said.

"Don't stress, you'll be covered," Blue said.

"Okay. Uh, guys, I'll see you soon." In other words, do not leave me alone long with Blue. Because seriously, what the heck was that about? Sure, Blue had flirted before, but he'd never made contact with me.

After the front door closed, I gulped. Now I was in a house alone with yet another hot biker, but he wasn't the one who was going to get the green-means-go sign into my panties.

"Blue—"

"No. Don't say anything. I just want you to know, before and *if* you and Talon take this further, I want my chance. I need you to know that Talon wasn't the only one watching you. What makes me different is that while I was watching, I wasn't doing anyone else. I think you're incredible, Zara. I want you in every way." He laid a kiss on my cheek and went over to the couch, sat down, and turned on the television.

Oh. My. God. What in the hell was that? No way, no flipping way. Blue wanted me? In every way?

Wait. What did he mean by while he was watching me, he wasn't doing anyone else? Did that mean Talon had?

Oh, who was I kidding? Of course he had. I witnessed myself his whoring-ness.

I shook my head to clear it. I didn't have time for this;

I had enough on my mind. If I let that get to me, I'd be sitting in a corner rocking back and forth, sucking my thumb.

"I'm going to clean. Yeah, cleaning is good."

Blue looked around the house. "Everything seems clean to me, baby."

"No, no, it isn't." I walked over to the couch and pointed to the carpet. "Look, can you see the crumbs?"

He leaned over, smiled, and said, "Nope."

"They're there." I got to my hands and knees, shoving my head down nearly into the carpet. "See there? It's really crummy."

Blue laughed. "Sure, baby. Clean away."

I got up, harrumphed, and added, "I have to dust first."

BY MID-AFTERNOON, I had dusted, cleaned the bathrooms and bedrooms, and vacuumed. Now, I was in the kitchen making Blue and myself sandwiches for a late lunch. I felt kind of terrible I hadn't offered him anything before that time, so to make it up to him, he was not only getting two sandwiches, but a piece of chocolate mud cake, a coffee, and a soft drink. I placed them all on a tray and took them into the lounge where his behind was still planted on the couch. Blue was now laughing at *Judge Judy* on TV.

"Wow, baby, maybe I should have confessed my devotion for you a long time ago if this is what I'm going to get."

I blushed and stuttered, "U-uh, no. I mean, I'm sorry for not...for being busy all morning and forgetting lunch. Um, no devotion needed here." I nodded and went back into the kitchen where my own lunch was waiting to be consumed.

I'd just sat down at the table when the phone rang. "Hello?" I answered.

"Why the frig have you not called me yet?" Deanna quietly hissed into the phone.

"Why would I call you at work?"

"Your brother and his partner popped in for a visit. They laughed at me 'cause I was as sweet as pie, no matter what they did; but then they informed me that Blue was all up in your face this morning. What happened?"

"Um, I can't talk right now."

"The fuck you can't...oh, I am so sorry, but I do not believe that is an option for you." I laughed. Someone must have walked into the library to cause Deanna to change her tune like that. On another hiss, she added, "Unless you want me to tell Maya about that time we smoked a joint when she was a baby and you ended up laughing so hard you cried 'cause you thought you had an ugly ape baby, you had better start talking."

That was a bit uncalled for. Not every baby was cute,

and it just happened that Maya was one of them; didn't mean I loved her less.

"Jeesh, all right. Hang on a sec'." Taking my plate with me, I got up and walked out to the lounge, where Blue gave me a knowing smirk. "Uh, I gotta take this. Be back." And I quickly headed down the hall to my bedroom. "You ready?" I asked into the phone after sitting down near the pillows on my bed.

"What do you think? Hurry it up, woman, before I get a customer."

"Okay, the quick low down. Blue came in, walked up to me, ran his hand down my cheek and said 'morning, baby.' Mattie and Julian left. Then—oh, my God, Deanna, then he confessed that Talon wasn't the only one watching me for two years. So had he. And he wants me in every way."

"Holy David Hasselhoff!" Deanna yelled. "Sorry, sorry." I knew she was apologizing to people at the library. "Heck, Zee. What are you going to do?" she whispered.

"Nothing."

"What do you mean, nothing?"

"Deanna, hun, he isn't the one who gets my heart and loins racing when he walks into a room. Sure, he's great looking, but...my-my heart already knows who it wants. Even if that guy can be a bossy, alpha-male arse sometimes. He's all of those things and mine."

Silence on the other end. That was never good coming from Deanna.

"Deanna?"

"That's good, Zee. I'm glad for you. Look, I gotta go. See ya later, loser." She sounded deflated, or her boss had just caught her on the phone once again.

"Yeah, okay, I'll see you later." When we'd have a serious talk.

After we'd hung up, I dropped the phone to the bed; a second later it rang again. I answered it with a chirpy, "Hello."

Nothing but air on the other end.

"Hello?" I said again.

Zilch reply.

"Look, if this is one of those heavy-breathing idiots, go out and get a job."

Still nothing.

My bedroom door was flung open. Talon stood there, breathing hard. Two steps and he had the phone out of my hand and had ended the call.

"Hey!" I glared.

"Kitten." He closed his eyes and breathed deeply. Upon opening them, he pulled me from the bed and wrapped his arms around me, then whispered, "It was him."

I froze. Somehow, I knew who he meant, and it certainly wasn't a random pervert.

"No." I shook my head against his chest.

"I asked Violet to hook me up," he said, still whispering. "We have your lines covered; you call out, we know who you're calling. We can hear the conversation. Anyone who calls in and says nothing, we trace their number. He had the balls to use his own phone."

"Talon," I whispered.

"He won't get to you. I promise."

He was telling the truth, but I was still scared out of my mind.

"Let it roll off you, kitten. Don't let him win."

Again, all I could do was nod.

"What's goin' on?" A concerned Blue asked from the doorway.

"Nothin' to concern you, *brother,*" Talon growled. He turned us both so we were facing Blue.

"I think it does, brother. I'm here to help, aren't I?"

"I think you're fuckin' here for other reasons, like hittin' on my woman."

My eyes widened. Blue looked at me. Did he think I said something?

"I-I never..."

"It's all right, baby." He smiled at me and turned a glare on Talon. "The phone call, right?" he asked.

Oh, crapola. Talon's words came rushing back to me. *We have your lines covered.* He had heard everything I'd said to Deanna.

"Yes," Talon snapped through clenched teeth. "But something you didn't hear, and that Zara would never share, 'cause she wouldn't wanna hurt you, was that you aren't the one who makes her heart race when you walk into a room. She already knows who she wants, and it ain't fuckin' you."

"Talon." I gasped because he was right. I would never have told Blue that.

"What, babe? At least I didn't mention anything about your loins." He chuckled. I buried my head in my hands and cringed.

"Well, congratu-fuckin'-lations."

I stood straight, my hand reached out to Blue.

"Blue—"

"It's all right, sweetheart."

"No, it ain't. Brothers don't do that shit to each other. A brother never goes after what's already another brother's. You knew I'd claimed Zara. What the fuck?"

"Come on, Talon. Look at her. She's one sweet piece in every way. Most bitches around our area only want one thing, a cock to lay on and get off. I'm sick of that crap. I want more, and I saw that in Zara. I knew I was too late; I could see it in her eyes the way she looks at you. But you can't hate me too much for trying."

"We'll fuckin' see. Right now, we got other stuff to deal with. Get back to the compound. I'm takin' *my* woman to get her kid."

“I get it, Talon, loud and clear.”

“Blue—”

“Don’t stress, baby. ‘S’all good.”

I nodded, looked at the floor, and without thinking—but feeling—I quietly said, “One day someone will come along, Blue, and you’ll know she’s it. She’ll do something that will blow your mind, and then she’ll be stuck there, and not a minute will go by that you won’t think about her. But that isn’t me, and I’m sorry.”

“Fuck,” he hissed. “See what I’m talkin’ ‘bout, brother? She’s got class, balls—especially to stand up to you—and sweetness. A total package.”

“I know that, brother,” Talon said. “Why’d you think I stopped stuffin’ around and grabbed her while I could? I’m just lucky enough she’s willin’ to grab me back.”

I pulled my lips between my teeth so I wouldn’t cry. This was a wonderful moment in my life.

It wouldn’t be until much later that I remembered about the phone call.

CHAPTER ELEVEN

Blue left just as Mattie and Julian arrived home with their arms filled with groceries. It was lucky they had the help of Vic, another of Talon's guys, to carry it all in. Vic had short blond hair, blue eyes, and was tall and slim, though you could tell he'd still hold his own in a fight. Or if he couldn't, he'd probably scare a bloke with the permanent scowl he had going on. Though, I wasn't entirely sure that scowl was permanent; it could have been there because Mattie and Julian had tortured him all day, dragging him here and there.

"The sex shop was the funniest." Julian cackled, just before Talon and I walked out the front door to collect Maya from school. Talon found that hilarious, whereas I found it worrisome. Because if it weren't for me and my…situation, Vic wouldn't have been put in that spot in the first place.

Poor Vic, he'll end up hating me.

"Kitten," Talon said as I walked quietly beside him.

"Yeah?" I looked over at him.

"Wanna talk 'bout your loins and how they race for me?"

I blushed, pulled my hand free of his, and shoved him. "No, jerk. Want to talk about the fact that you didn't mention doing anything to my phone in the first place?"

"No. I'm glad I didn't. Or I wouldn't have found out what your heart already wanted…me."

"Yeah, right. I was actually talking about the postman. Hoo-wee, he gets me going."

Talon stopped and whipped me into his arms. "Don't. Don't joke about this, kitten. I may be teasin', but I'm so fuckin' full to the brim with…gratefulness to hear that come outta your mouth. You had me worried that I was the only one feeling this, but now I know I'm not, and it makes me happy for the first time in a hell of a long time."

"Talon—"

It was then, in the middle of the street, not far from Maya's school, that he kissed me. And it wasn't only lust riding the kissable train that time, but some feelings had jumped aboard as well.

It was magical.

WE STOOD out the front of Maya's class, receiving a lot of stares. Mainly because I had never shown up to collect Maya with a male before, and the way Talon hugged me to his front, it was undeniable that we weren't just friends.

That was when I saw Maya—who was usually the first one out— come out last with the teacher following her.

"Uh-oh," I said.

"Relax, babe. Can't be that bad. Maya's a good kid."

"Hmm." *We'll see about that.* He had never been with her down the street when she wasn't getting what she wanted. I swear she'd become possessed by the devil.

"Hi, Miss Edgingway," Mrs Faith said with a sigh.

"What's wrong?" I asked though she wasn't looking at me. Even when she greeted me, her eyes were on Talon. Did he have that effect on all ages? Because I was sure Mrs Faith was at least sixty.

"Um—"

And she'd never done that before; I didn't think 'um' was in her vocabulary.

She shook her head and focused back on me. "Do you mind if we have a word alone for a minute?"

"Sure. Maya, honey, why don't you go and show Talon the play area?"

"Okay, Momma." She pulled my sleeve so I was eye-to-eye with her. "Just remember it was real important I done what I done." With that, she spun away, grabbed Talon's hand, and skipped off while Talon walked beside her to the play equipment.

A moment later, I realised I wasn't the only one enjoying the view. Though, *I* wasn't staring at Talon's butt like Mrs Faith was. I was admiring how great it looked for Maya to have Talon beside her, as he looked down listening to something she was saying and then burst out laughing.

I cleared my throat. "Sooo," I started.

"Yes, I am sorry to tell you this, but we had an incident today that involved Maya. We don't condone violence at this school; and honestly, I was shocked that your daughter decided to use such force when she got angry at another student. I have had words with her, and I am sure you will as well. Please make sure that she will not head down that path again."

"What actually happened?"

"Maya hit another child in the stomach, quite hard actually. She didn't like something the other student had said to her. Of course, we both know that even if she doesn't like something, it should never come to violence to get her message across."

"Yes, of course. And I will be speaking to her about the matter this afternoon. I am terribly sorry for what has happened. But, um, can I ask what was said?"

"I think I will leave that up to Maya to inform you. Have a good weekend, Miss Edgingway."

"Yes. Uh, thank you, Mrs Faith."

She turned and scuttled off into her classroom. Old stuffy bat; I was sure it wasn't as bad as it sounded.

I sighed. Time to find out what my little monster had done. I walked around the corner and saw red. Talon was standing by the side of the play equipment watching Maya being a monkey, swinging from one bar to another. That was fine. What I didn't like was *what* was standing by Talon. Okay, maybe I shouldn't say what; it was a she. Stacey MacDonald. The sluttiest of all sluts. And okay, maybe I shouldn't say that, because I hardly knew the lady, but I'd heard enough about her. All the mothers talked about how much she flirted with all the fathers and male teachers at the school. And right now, she was running a hand down Talon's arm, and they were laughing at something she'd just said.

I stalked over, walked around her to Talon's other side, and wrapped my arms around his middle.

"Oh, Zara. Hi."

I grinned but glared. "Yeah, hi, Stacey." I turned my gaze to Talon and gentled my look. "You ready to go, honey?"

He smirked, his lips twitching. Was he seriously fighting not to laugh right now?

"Sure, kitten. Maya, we're goin'."

"Okay," Maya called. She knew she was about to get into trouble because usually, it would take me calling her at least five times before she listened.

Stacey cleared her throat. "Right, bye, Zara. Talon, I'll see you around some time."

WTF?

"Um, no. I don't think you will, Stacey. I plan on keeping Talon very busy for a *very* long time."

She rolled her eyes. "Sure, Zara."

I shook my head, grabbed Talon's hand in mine, and took Maya's hand within the other and left.

Stupid, slutty wench.

Talon leaned into me and whispered, "Do you wanna piss on me as well, kitten?" Then he chuckled.

"Not funny, Talon."

"What's not funny, Ma?"

"Nothing, honey. Now, any chance you want to tell me what happened today?"

She groaned. "I had to do it, Momma. Toby was being mean."

"Maya, what was Toby saying or doing that was so bad to receive a punch in the stomach?"

Talon chuckled. I elbowed him in the ribs and sent him my evil glare. He shut up, but a grin stayed upon his lips.

"It was my turn for news—"

"Yes." I nodded. "And you showed everyone that *Monster High* doll, right?"

"Yeah, but I also had way better news than that."

"And?" I prompted.

"I told the class I had a daddy now." I gasped. Talon's hand in mine grew tighter. "Toby said Talon wasn't my daddy, just someone my mum was dating. I thought he was not right. He was yelling that he was, and said I was silly for even thinkin' it. So I punched him."

Oh, dear.

Not knowing what to say, I decided to steer clear of that whole dad topic—leave it for when I had some inspirational answers, which always came after a bottle of scotch.

So I moved on to the lecture of not hurting anyone, even if they think they were right and were vocal about it. Maya then stomped off up the front steps after I took her hour of television privileges away for the night. In other words—her world had ended. Maya wasn't the only one I didn't want to talk to about the dad subject. As soon as I was in the front door, I headed for the kitchen where I could hear Mattie and Julian.

"All right, where are we at with dinner? Because a roast takes a while, and then there's all the other preparing to do with the vegetables."

"Did you smoke a joint while you were out?" Mattie

asked. I was shocked that came out of his mouth; usually, he was more reserved.

To prove my shock, my eyes bulged, and my mouth dropped open. "No, I did not."

He turned to Julian and said, "Something happened on the way home."

Julian nodded. "Oh, definitely."

I didn't get to respond because Talon walked into the kitchen with his phone to his ear.

"Right," he barked. "Well, drop him at the compound." He ran a hand through his hair. "I'll be there. What time? That's none of your business. Well, I could just come and get him like it was fuckin' planned, woman." He sighed. "Christ, fine."

"Talon?" I asked. He was very agitated.

"Stupid bitch. I was supposed to go and grab Cody. But she's bringing him here."

I stiffened. "As in here, here?"

"Nah, kitten, across the road. I wouldn't wanna burden you with that slut. I'll be back soon. No one leaves the house. I'll have guys watching, but no one leaves. Got it?"

"Sure thang, Spiderman." Julian saluted. Mattie nodded.

Without thinking, my body went to Talon. I curled my arms around his waist and met his gaze. He was annoyed, and I wanted to make him better. "Sorry, she's made you mad, honey."

His eyes softened. "You doin' what you just did, and saying what you just said, made putting up with her a whole lot easier. 'Preciate it, kitten. Now kiss me."

And I did.

It started out slow, a touch of lips. But as soon as Talon's tongue touched my bottom lip, I dove, and it soon got hot and heavy.

"They should charge money for this. It's nearly like porn, but they're clothed," Julian commented.

I pulled away and smiled at Talon, his eyes showed he was amused, but his mouth frowned, and he grumbled, "One fuckin' day, kitten."

CHAPTER TWELVE

An hour and a half later, dinner was ready, but it was still keeping warm in the oven while we waited for Talon and Cody. Deanna had turned up and was sitting in front of the turned-off television with Maya, playing with her *Monster High* dolls. Mattie was at the table reading the paper while Julian sat beside him reading something on his iPad. I was checking the kitchen floor for any uneven ground as I walked back and forth over it.

That was when we all heard yelling out the front. I looked at the guys at the table as they looked at me. We bolted for the lounge.

"Maya, baby, come to your room and show me all your *Lalaloopsy* dolls," Mattie said.

"Sure, Uncle Mattie." Maya, none the wiser—at least I hoped not—ran off to her room with Mattie following.

Deanna, Julian, and I were just about to peek out the front curtain when we heard, "I should at least get the chance to meet your new whore before she plays house with *my* son."

"Bianca, just fuckin' leave. Hell, it's none of your business who I'm doin'."

Well, really. He hasn't even done me yet.

"Holy shit," Deanna said, grinning. I hadn't had a chance to speak to her...okay, I had a chance, but she ignored said chances to talk in private.

There was a knock at the front door. "Open up, bitch!"

"Mum," I heard Cody hiss in a whisper.

Oh. My. God. She was acting like this in front of her son. That was just...disgraceful.

I opened the door to witness Talon grab his ex by the arm and pull her roughly away from the door.

"Honey," I said with a buttery-sweet tone and a smile on my face. "Don't go doing that, I would love to meet... Bianca, wasn't it?"

Bianca looked at me from head to toe with a sneer on her face. She was beautiful. I could understand why Talon had married her. She had long blonde hair, light blue eyes, and a slim body that was wrapped up in designer gear.

I was sure I looked a treat, too. "Sorry, if I'd known I was receiving company, I would have spruced up a little. I've been cleaning all day."

"You clean your own house."

It wasn't a question, it was more of a disgusted statement.

Deanna stepped forward from behind the door. "No, woman, fairies fly outta her ass and they do it for her."

Cody laughed, but he quickly hid it behind a cough when his mum glared at him.

"Hey, Cody." I waved. He smiled. "Why don'cha come on in. Julian will take you to meet Maya."

"Bye, Mum," he whispered as he walked past her into the house, only to stop just inside when his mum spoke.

"Now hang on a second, bitch!" She turned to Talon. "I don't want him stayin' here with one of your pieces of pussy."

"My time with my boy, I do what I want. And if spending that time is with *my* woman, it's fuckin' what we'll do."

With hands on my hips, I said, "Talon, honey. Check your language in front of the kids."

Talon looked at me with a smile on his face. "Right, kitten."

Bianca gasped.

"Come on, little Thor. Let's leave these cats to hiss it

out," Julian said, and with a gentle hand on Cody's shoulder, he ushered him forward and down the hall.

"You are fucking shitting me!" Bianca screeched.

I stepped out the door with Deanna behind me and closed it. I'd had enough. I turned to Bianca with a glare.

"I would appreciate it if you would be more civilised around my house. I do not condone bad language when my daughter is present. Now, I am not trying to replace you in any way when it concerns Cody. All I wanted was to meet and get to know *my* man's child. I'm sorry if that hurts you in some way, but if this *is* what Talon wants, then I will stand by him."

She looked from Talon to me. "You have got to be kidding me. This? That is what you're fucking choosing to screw? Some toffee fat bitch?"

"Watch what you fuckin' say, Bianca."

"Yeah, right, you won't do anything about it, 'cause you know you'd lose Cody."

Holy heck. She was really going to play that card with him?

"Now that's just uncalled for," I said.

She took a step toward me. "I don't give a fuck what you have to say or think, bitch."

Deanna started bouncing up and down on the balls of her feet beside me. "Oh, come on, come on. Let me at her. Talon? Zara? Please."

Bianca looked to Deanna. "And who the fuck are you?"

Deanna ignored the question and looked to Talon with pleading eyes. "Please."

Talon chuckled. "If it's okay with Zara, have at it, Hell Mouth."

Deanna begged me with her eyes. I would have loved to have said my piece, but I didn't want the children to overhear. I didn't want to cause Talon any more damage, and I thought if it didn't come from me, then the problem wouldn't escalate. Also, Deanna sure did have a way with words, and when she wanted to get a certain message across, she did, with a firework result.

And who was I to spoil her fun? I nodded at Deanna.

She beamed, stepped in front of me, and snarled in Bianca's face, "Don't you ever fuckin' come here giving shit to my sista and her man. I will fuckin' take you down, slut. I'm not a pulling hair, sissy fighta. I claw, bite, and give my all, and there is a lot. And if you even think of holding Cody against Talon, I will rip you and your life apart. You think you got money and you can do or say anything? Well, shit, woman, I got so much money I could use it as toilet paper. So, I have every chance to fuck you and your husband over. Now back the fuck up, woman, and leave. Let them have this. If you don't, I'll rain down on you faster than you can blink."

Bianca did indeed blink...and then again. She opened

her mouth, shut it and then stuttered, "B-but—" She shook her head and stood straighter. "Hang on a sec, she just swore."

I shrugged and said, "Yeah, but she was quiet about it. The kids wouldn't have heard that."

"What-fucking-ever." She turned and went down the steps, then left.

"Honey, your ex is a…not a nice person," I said as we stared after her.

Deanna sighed. "Zee, she's a bitch."

"That she is, Hell Mouth, and so much more. But I think you just scared the fuck outta her. So, thanks," Talon said.

"Not a problem, bossman. I enjoyed it."

Talon took the steps two at a time and was in front of me, then I was in his arms. "Sorry 'bout that, kitten."

I wrapped my arms around his waist and grinned up at him. "Don't apologise for that thing, honey. I just hope we can salvage dinner."

"What did I ever do to deserve you?" Talon grinned.

"And me," Deanna said.

Talon chuckled. "Yeah, Hell Mouth, and fuckin' you. Let's go eat, babe."

DINNER WASN'T TOO BAD. The meat was still tender

enough that we didn't have to carve it with a chainsaw. Maya adored Cody, and I think the feeling was mutual. Cody didn't say much while we ate, but he did smile, and of course laughed at Deanna and Julian a lot. Though, who wouldn't?

After checking with Cody first, we set up a bed in Maya's room; she was over the moon to have company. I hoped she didn't talk his ears off. Talon's only comment was that I needed a bigger house. I laughed and said I liked it the way it was. That was when he informed me that tomorrow we were staying at his house with the kids because at least there the walls were more soundproof and he could have his wicked way with me. I gulped.

It wasn't until Julian and Mattie had gone to bed, Deanna had left with Griz, complaining all the way, and Talon and I were in bed and asleep—after fooling around for a bit—that I woke in the middle of the night from a nightmare about *the* phone call. If Talon hadn't been there, it would have advanced into a full-blown panic attack.

"Like I said, kitten," Talon whispered, "we're going to my house tomorrow; not for the other reasons, but 'cause it's safer. I have an alarm system and cameras. We'll take everyone if we have to. I'll keep you safe, babe. Always."

"Okay, honey," I said. Because I knew that was true.

CHAPTER THIRTEEN

"Momma, Mum, Ma. Mummy, wake up."

I woke up wishing my daughter had a snooze button like my alarm clock. She didn't, of course, so I had to pry open my eyes and pay attention to her.

"Yes, Maya, my wonderful, pain-in-the-beehive daughter. What is so important to wake me up on a Saturday morning?"

"I'm hungry."

Seriously? Where was that duct tape when I needed it? I sat up slowly, looked next to me, and found the bed empty. Well, there went my morning nookie.

Wait. Where in the heck did that come from?

Why was I thinking about nookie in the first place with my daughter present?

That damn Talon.

"Maya, was that all you needed, hun?" Because last I knew, we had a house full of people who could have helped her out; and also, from the sound of it, they were *already* awake.

"No. I've got swimming, remember?" She smiled.

I glanced at the clock and hissed, "Snap." I threw the covers back; thankfully, I was wearing my PJs, so I bounced off the bed and ordered, "Right, Maya, get dressed, get the bag from the laundry with a towel in it, and be ready. I'll throw some clothes on, and we'll get going. Okay?"

"Okay." She ran from the room, yelling, "We're late, we're late."

We weren't that late. Swimming started in ten minutes and we lived five minutes away by car from the centre. Okay, so maybe we were going to be a little late, but we had to go; my little-uncoordinated angel needed as many lessons as possible.

I dressed in black leggings, a tight long-sleeved black top under a looser fitting tee that read 'This ain't no milk store'. I slipped on a pair of combat boots and ran from my room to the kitchen where Talon and Cody already were.

"Gotta go, gotta go, people," I said, as I quickly filled a travel mug of coffee. I was about to walk out of the kitchen and yell at Maya to get her beehive out here when Talon called, "Kitten."

"Yes, honey?" I turned to face him. "Oh, sorry. Morning, Cody. I hope you've had breakfast. Hey, do you want to come with us? I'm sure Maya would love to show you how not to swim while trying to learn to swim."

Cody beamed and looked from me to Talon, so I moved my gaze to Talon also.

"Kitten, get your arse over here."

I sighed and rolled my eyes. "Talon, I don't have time for this. I need to go. Maya!" I yelled.

"Comin'!" she yelled back.

"Kitten." There was a tone of warning in his voice.

I sighed. "Yes, Talon?"

"Get your arse over here. Kiss me, and then you can go. I'll bring Cody with me in a moment; I gotta see to something at the compound."

"Oh, okay." I grinned, walked over to him, and gave him a quick peck on the mouth. Talon wasn't having any of that. As I went to pull away, he brought me closer and really kissed me, so thoroughly that my legs went wonky and my fandola sang "Let's Get it On." Then I remembered we had an audience.

I stepped away and glared at him. "Talon," I snapped. "None of that in front of Cody—"

"He don't mind."

"That's beside the point. I do not neck in front of our children."

His eyes went extra soft. What had I done or said to receive that response from him? I wasn't sure, but I knew I liked it.

Though, then I remembered. "And do not say the a-word again, mister," I said, jabbing him in the chest with my finger.

"Babe." He smiled. "Let's leave the cursing lesson till later when you're not going to be late."

I gasped, looked at the clock on the microwave, and yelled, "Maya, let's move it." I gave Talon a quick peck, Cody a hair ruffle, and over my shoulder, I said, "See you there."

Maya met me in the lounge. She said a quick goodbye and we left.

MAYA WAS in the pool room that was glassed off from the parents. I was in the sitting area watching through the glass, which I found was better for the children because they were able to concentrate on their teacher without having parents yelling orders. I also thought it was wonderful because it blocked out the noise of rowdy kids for half an hour. I was in the back row near the front door, so it was easier for me to keep an eye out for Talon and Cody while watching Maya.

I grimaced as Maya dove in—well, more belly-flopped in. I glanced over my shoulder once again to see some woman run out of the centre, when I spotted Cody walking through the door. I smiled and waved him over.

"Hey," I said as he sat down next to me.

"Hi," he whispered. Something was wrong.

"Um, Cody, are you okay?"

"Yeah."

Alrighty.

"Cody, where's your dad?"

He looked over his shoulder, and as he did, his top lip curled up in a look of disgust. "Coming," he said.

I looked behind me to see that Talon was coming in, but with him was a blonde-haired, blue-eyed, big-boobed bimbo. She was dressed in the tightest of tight jeans, where anyone could see her camel-toe and a tight white tee. I turned my attention front and centre and tried my best not to jump over the chair and rip her apart for touching my man. Unfortunately, they stopped too far behind us for me to be able to hear what they were saying.

"Who's that, buddy?" I asked Cody.

"Dunno. But don't worry, Zee. Dad likes you better." He looked at me with concerned eyes.

I smiled and patted his arm. "I know, bud."

Whoever she was, she had to go. It was making Cody uncomfortable and upset.

"Be back in a sec," I whispered to Cody. "Can you watch Maya for me?" I pointed her out. He didn't say anything, only nodded.

I got up, plastered a big smile on my face, and walked up to Talon and Pamela Anderson-wannabe.

Before she noticed me, I heard her whisper, "So, when are you gonna give me another chance to have that cock of yours?"

"Pam," Talon sighed. His eyes were on me as he added, "I already told you, I got a woman now—"

"I don't mind sharing. You know that." She smiled and leaned her tits into his arm.

I took a deep breath and stopped in front of them; she looked at me and glared. "Hi." I grinned. "I'm Zara Edgingway, Talon's woman. Can I ask that you refrain from rubbing up against *my* man? I don't like to see it, and his son doesn't like to see it. Actually, I find it disgusting that you would even act in such a way in front of these people. Do you have a child here?"

"Yes," she hissed.

"You better run and be a good mother then, instead of coming on to a man who already said he's taken, and acting like some dog in heat."

She stalked off without another word.

I glared up at Talon with my hands on my hips and

snapped, “I am seriously thinking of tattooing a sign on your forehead when you’re asleep that says ‘Property of Zara.’“ Then I walked off, leaving Talon chuckling behind me.

After Maya finished, we stood outside in the warm midmorning, waiting while Talon and Cody had a great laugh about what I’d said to Talon earlier. Cody was laughing his pants off. I was a little annoyed, but also happy to see Cody smile and laugh with his father, even if it was at my expense. Maya was standing silently beside me, only because she was chomping down a lollipop that Talon had bought her after swimming.

“All right, let’s get a-goin’. Babe, you gotta pack some stuff to take to my place.”

“Are we stayin’ at Talon’s?” Maya asked.

“If that’s okay with you.” I smiled down at her.

“That’d be cool. Cody was telling me all about it and how big it was; and, Momma, they got a Xbox *and* a Play-Station. I wanna try those.”

“I’m sure that would be fine.”

My daughter is easily bought.

“We’ll meet you back at the house,” I said, then turned to walk off, only my arm was caught on something, and that something pulled. I was spun back around and wrapped up in tight arms.

“When’re you gonna flippin’ learn?” Talon growled.

“Uh,” was my smart response.

"When one of us is leavin', kitten, I want your mouth. Now give it to me."

"And what did I say about necking in front of the kids?" I glared.

"They'll get used to it." He grinned and then proceeded to kiss me, and of course, once his mouth was on mine, my brain went blank and my body took over. Meaning, we were definitely necking in front of the kids.

He stopped the kiss, stepped back, smirked, and gave a chin lift to someone behind me. I turned to see one of Talon's biker brothers do the whole chin lift back. Only when I looked back at Talon, he was already on his way to his car with Cody.

"Ma, we going?"

"Yes, Maya."

We walked over to my car, a beat-up black Volkswagen Beetle, got in, and it was then that Maya informed me, "I like Talon for a daddy. He makes you smile a lot."

I bit my bottom lip, smiled at her and nodded. Pulling out of the car park, I noticed Talon's biker brother followed us all the way home. I should have noticed that morning that I had a tail, but I hadn't. Really, I should have been the one in the first place to have asked someone to follow or come with us in case anything happened. In case *he* had someone out there watching and waiting for the right moment to commence his payback, but I didn't think of it.

Why?

Because Talon makes me feel safe.

TALON and I walked in the front door at the same time, and at the looks on Julian, Mattie, and Deanna's faces, I wanted to walk right back out. Mattie quickly ushered Cody and Maya into Maya's room to play games. Then Griz walked out of the kitchen carrying a bunch of bright pink assorted flowers.

I looked at Talon. His body went solid beside me as his hand squeezed mine. "Did you buy me flowers?" I asked, though I already knew the answer, only I didn't want to admit it.

He shook his head.

I closed my eyes. "They're from him, aren't they?"

"There was a note, boss," Griz barked.

"Kitten, look at me."

I kept my eyes closed and shook my head. I didn't want to look at him. I didn't want to see the note, or the flowers, or the pity from anyone. I wanted to lock my family, friends, and myself away in an oblivious bubble and not think of anything.

"She's gonna blow," Deanna said.

And, in fact, she was right. I felt the pressure build, the stress and the heartache of not having enough time to mourn my parents, of having to deal with this prick again in my life. I was angry, pissed, annoyed and sexually frustrated.

I didn't realise I was still shaking my head until Talon captured it between his palms and tilted it. My eyes opened and saw he was just as furious as I was.

"You can't do this right now. I'd love to let you loose, but not now, and not here with the kids. Do not let this fucker win."

"I need something, Talon. I need to vent soon, honey, or I'm gonna go crazy."

"Girls' night!" Julian cried. I stepped out of Talon's hold and turned to him as he continued, "Or day, should I say. You need to vent, kidney bean; we'll do that in style. Drinking, massages, make-up, dancing, drinking, crying, screaming and drinking some more."

"I can't, Julian—"

Mattie emerged from the hallway saying, "No, it's a great idea. I can take care of the children. Zee, it would make you feel so much better."

"It's not right. Not now, I can't leave Maya and Cody alone. Not that they'd be alone... I just shouldn't."

"Babe, you should. Matthew can take the kids to my place with Vic, Bizz, and Stake. They'll be fuckin' safer there than anywhere." He looked to Griz and then back to me. "I got shit I need to do, but I'll catch up with you sometime. Until then, Griz, Blue, and Pick will be with you, Hell Mouth, and Julian."

"I—"

"No, kitten. Do this. You need an outlet. As much as I'd like you to fuckin' use me, that ain't gonna work right now. All right?"

I nodded. "Okay, honey."

He smiled brightly and said, "Good."

CHAPTER FOURTEEN

Talon left with the flowers and note—after, of course, a hot make-out session. And yes, it was in front of everyone. I was getting the impression he wasn't unfavourable toward public displays of affection. Something I was still learning to get over myself.

Maya and Cody were both fine with going to Talon's without me, and instead with Mattie and the bikers. I packed as Maya gabbed on about how unreal it was going to be staying at Talon's, that she was going to have a huge-arse—yes, she said arse, but only because Cody had—room to herself. I was going to have to have another word with Talon. Though, what had me forgiving Cody so quickly for cursing was when Maya told me that he'd said if she got scared through the night, she was allowed to go into his room, that he'd keep her safe.

Wasn't that just the cutest thing?

Before they left, I gave Cody a big hug for what he'd said.

It caused him to look at me strangely, because either he didn't know why, or he just wasn't used to a mother figure showing him affection.

Griz made himself at home on the couch, watching motorbike racing, while Deanna, Julian, and I sat at the kitchen table, organising the afternoon and night's events. We were arguing about whether cocktails or straight shots were going to be the main choice of beverage when the front door opened and in walked Blue and Pick. They sat down with Griz after a quick hello, and we went back to arguing while we made lunch for everyone.

In the end, we decided to do both. Once lunch was consumed—or wolfed away, where the men were concerned—Julian announced, "Massage time. Then we'll start a little drinky-poo."

"Whoa, hang on. I thought we were going somewhere for that massage," Deanna said.

Julian rolled his eyes. "Don't be silly, apple tart. I am actually a professional masseuse. I've got my table in my car and all. Girl, you won't know what hit you when I get my hands on you."

Julian, with the help of Griz, got his table from the car. Once we moved the lounge around a bit, we placed the table in the middle. None of the bedrooms were big enough to have it in.

The guys positioned themselves back on the couch and chair and continued to watch television. That was until Deanna came out in my robe. I had demanded—because it was my night—that she went first.

"Okay, lemon drop, lie on your stomach." Julian patted his table.

Deanna turned a glare on the guys, who quickly looked away, then lay down. She had Julian help her remove my robe so that all she was left wearing was her low-riding jeans. Her top half was naked. Not that you could see anything, thank goodness, or I wouldn't be getting up there. Julian squirted some oil onto his hands and rubbed them together. As soon as he placed them on Deanna's back and started to work out her knots, she moaned low in her throat.

"Jesus," Griz growled.

I grinned.

"I think I'm in the wrong job," Pick said.

I looked to Blue. He wasn't looking at Deanna at all. His eyes were on me, and once I'd turned to him, he said, "Looking forward to your turn, babe."

I blushed and had second thoughts about actually having a go.

"Blue," Griz barked.

Blue smirked and shrugged at Griz. "Can't help myself," he said.

Julian worked Deanna for half an hour, then wrapped the robe back around her; as she got up from the table, her eyes were hooded. That was when I noticed Griz adjust himself in his pants. He so wanted her.

"Come on, French fry, your turn," Julian said to me.

"Um, no. I think I'll be all right." I gave him a small smile.

"If I had to do it, so do fuckin' you," Deanna called from my room, where she was probably getting ready to shower to remove the oil from her skin.

"Unless you want me to do it, baby," Blue said.

"You are just askin' for it, dickhead," Griz snapped.

"It could be the only chance I'll get to have my hands on her sweet skin," Blue commented like it meant nothing, his eyes on me while my eyes were wide and worried.

Griz elbowed him in the ribs and ordered, "Get your stupid arse outside. Wildcat don't need that shit." He turned back to Blue. "And Talon will fuckin' kill you if you make this night crap for her."

Blue flinched. "Sorry, babe." He got up from the couch and left out the front door.

"Don't worry, Zara, he'll be all right. He'll still help out tonight," Pick said.

Was I right to feel bad for Blue? A part of me said no,

and then another part said yes. What I didn't understand —even though they'd said some nice things about me— and couldn't comprehend, was that both Talon and Blue thought that I was an okay type of gal.

Maybe they were high most of the time?

That was all I had to explain their interest in me.

AN HOUR LATER, I had worked out that Julian was actually a god, and I wanted to chop off his hands and sell them on eBay. I could have made millions. But because I couldn't do that, I had a shower after my near-orgasmic massage, and was now dressed in a long black skirt, combat boots, and a black tee that read 'Rock On'. I put some make-up on and gunk in my hair to control the frizz. I piled it up, with the help of many bobby pins, on the top of my head—only Julian had to have his way and place a few ringlets hanging down. He was dressed in dark blue jeans and a teal-coloured shirt. Deanna looked amazing in tight black pants and a silky grey shirt. What we were dressed up for, I didn't have a clue, but once I started on my third cocktail, I didn't care. It was while I was on that third cocktail and fifth shot that I broke down crying when Julian mentioned my parents. Then I went from grieving to flat-out pissed off.

To say the least, I was so happy I had Deanna and

Julian there to fuel my fire inside. We yelled and screamed. I quivered a bit and then whispered my worries to them both as we sat at the kitchen table.

Then I announced, "You know what? We missin' one of me gals 'ere. I'm gonna ring Vi."

"We 'on't need dat bitch," Deanna said. She was a little drunk.

Okay, we all were.

"Deanna," I sighed. "Honey lumpkin, you need to learn to play nice with others. I lov' ya, but life is all 'bout expanding. Look at me, I have a hot biker boyfriend, who I so want to have sex with—"

"Fuckin' hell," Griz growled from the lounge room.

"You said it, brother," Blue griped.

"They're kinda funny," Pick said.

"Don't listen in then, punks," Deanna yelled at them.

"Yeah!" Julian yelled as well and then, "Go on, cock ring, and ring her."

Julian's cute pet names, I noticed once he was drunk, turned dirty.

I reached for the phone on the kitchen bench and said, "All right, I'm gonna do it." *After a long drink of water.*

I rang her mobile number; on the third ring, she picked up.

"'Lo," she said

"Why 'ello there, Miss Marcus. You know I really

should have taken notice of your last name more because it's just like Talon's."

"Zara?"

"Yeah?"

"Are you drunk?" I could hear the smile in her voice.

"Maybe a wee little bit, and I thought, I'm having a few drinks with Deanna and Julian, and I was missing someone, and that someone was you. Now get your behind here and drink with us," I ordered.

"I doubt Barbie wants me there—"

"Oh, don't mind her, she's all full of shit bein' a hater."

"No, I'm not," Deanna yelled beside me. I shoved her. She teetered in her chair, about to fall—and I would have laughed my arse off—but then she regained her balance.

"I can't, anyway," Violet said. "I'm still at work, and I've got some filing to finish."

"Hmm." I thought for a second and then slapped the table with my hand. "I've got it. We'll come to you."

"Yay, an outing. Ooh, I've got to get my shoes." Julian ran from the kitchen, yelling, "Has anyone seen my shoes? We're going out."

"Like fuck," Griz barked.

"I don't think you should do that, Zee. Someone doesn't sound happy about it on your end," Vi said.

"Oh, pish posh. Leave them to me. See you soon, hun, and we'll bring some grog." I hung up before she could complain about my idea.

Griz, Pick, and Blue stomped into the kitchen. They all looked good enough to eat, standing there in jeans, biker boots, tight tees and their Hawks vests, with their arms crossed over their chests.

"You know," I began, "you guys are pretty good looking."

"You ain't charming us into doin' this shit, Wildcat," Griz said. His dark blue gaze shifted from me to Deanna and narrowed.

"What? Don't look like that at me; it wasn't my idea. Still, it's a good one. We need to get out. No, scratch that, Zee needs to get out, have stress-fuckin'-free fun. It's what her bossman would want for her."

"Hey, yeah. Good point there." I nodded. "Call my sex-on-legs man. See what he says."

Griz stalked into the lounge; his voice was low enough we couldn't hear what was being said, but he sounded outraged. Looked to me like I was going to get my way. I grinned.

"Hell, baby, this is a bad idea, but you knew Talon'd let this fly for you," Blue commented.

I shrugged and tried not to look so pleased.

"Makes me kind of thankful it ain't me dealing with this shit. If you were my woman, I wouldn't allow this."

I bit my bottom lip.

"Nah, I'm still fucking jealous." He walked off as Griz came in.

"Let's roll then." He turned to Pick. "Go get your vehicle, you and Blue follow—"

Julian ran into the room saying, "Found them, thunder cunts. They were under the bed."

"Julian Jacob, do not say that word around me again," I snapped.

"Sorry, pussy flaps." He smiled sweetly. I rolled my eyes, and Deanna burst out laughing.

"You three are with me," Griz ordered.

Excitement ran through my body. I couldn't keep still in the car on the way to work, which wasn't far. Really, we could have walked, but I wasn't going to push that idea. Deanna sat in the front of the tough-looking black Chrysler, next to Griz; Julian was in the back with me. We kept looking at each other, smiling and giggling.

We pulled up to the office, and I got out juggling a bottle of tequila, a bottle of bourbon, and a cocktail shaker. Julian was carrying the glasses for us to use because I knew there were none at the office, well, besides coffee cups. But that just wasn't going to happen.

Griz came around the front of the car and barked, "Next time, you wait till I'm outta the car and the boys have pulled up and got out as well."

"Sorry, Griz," I said in a little girl's voice. Julian and Deanna laughed. Griz's eyes narrowed.

It turned out to be a great idea of mine. Violet was a great person usually, but a hoot when she was tipsy. We were surrounding her desk, sitting in our own chairs, talking and laughing about our first time experiences in sex. The guys were sitting back a bit, pretending not to listen as they played cards.

"It wasn't until I met Travis that I was introduced to receiving it hard. God, I loved it when he used to pound into me and let me tell you, he was huge. Delicious." Vi licked her lips and grinned at the memory.

"Christ," Blue swore.

"I think I need a smoke after that," Julian said. We all laughed.

"What about you, Barbie?"

"The best time I've ever had sex was when—"

"Enough," Griz growled. "I don't wanna hear any more of this shit."

"Aw, but we haven't got to my turn yet," Julian moaned.

"No offense, man, but we had to hear about your first time; that was enough," Pick said.

"You know what?" I asked the room.

Vi, Deanna, and Julian all asked "What?" at the same time, causing us to laugh again.

"I need music."

"Yeah, that'd be a grand idea. I want to dance." Violet

smiled, but then it quickly faded. “But I haven’t got anything here to listen to it on.”

“Not even a radio?” Julian asked.

“Nope. But hey, there’s a bar just down the road—”

“Fuck no,” Blue said.

“Yes. Yes, I like that idea.” I clapped. “Come on, guys, it’s just down the road, like five places away. We can walk. Nothing’s gonna happen.”

CHAPTER FIFTEEN

We walked into the bustling bar. The atmosphere felt great, with dim lighting and someone singing at the karaoke machine. The pool tables were full; so were the booths and seating area at the bar.

Deanna dragged me over to the bar and squeezed her way in, shouting out to the bar girl in a tight white tee that she wanted four shots of Cock Sucking Cowboys.

Upon paying, she dished out the shots and on the count of three, down they went and up came my hamburger from dinner…nearly.

"Oh, I love this song. Let's dance," Julian shouted when Taylor Swift's "Trouble" came through the karaoke machine, and some young girl started singing it with a not-too-bad voice.

We left Griz, Pick, and Blue at the bar, while Violet, Deanna, Julian and I went to shake our booties.

Two songs later, I glanced around for our guards, only they were no longer brooding at the bar. I looked around, but couldn't see them anywhere. Violet tugged on my arm, and while she jiggled what her mama gave her, she pointed through the crowd to a booth in the far corner where they were now seated—still brooding. Their arms were crossed over their chests and their eyes said 'don't speak to me or I'll bite your head off.'

It was only Griz's gaze that lasered into us. Though, I think that had something to do with the way Deanna was grinding against some innocent young man…um, okay, maybe he wasn't that innocent, considering the way he grabbed her boobs. I giggled to myself when she elbowed him in the ribs and pushed him away. She turned her gaze to me, grinned and shook her head.

Deanna, Julian, and I made our way to the table while Vi went to grab us some more drinks. I'd asked for water because I didn't think my stomach could handle another toxic mix. That was when Deanna called me a pussy and said to Vi that if she got me water, they'd be having words. Violet then proceeded to laugh in Deanna's face, and answered with 'Whatever.' I knew what I'd be getting —water.

I collapsed next to Pick. Griz and Blue stood so Julian and Deanna could sit, and then Vi when she got back. It was like they were protecting the President's daughter. Blue and Griz had their backs to us; both were standing straight and still, glaring out at the partygoers.

Wow, they must take their jobs seriously.

"You know, I kind of feel like Whitney Houston in *Bodyguard* right now," Julian said

I held up my fist to be pumped and yelled, "That's what I was just thinking." *Sort of.* Why I was yelling I had no clue; it wasn't so hard to hear in our corner.

"Yo, Vi. Oh, my God, I love you," I yelled—yes, again—when she deposited a bottle of water in front of me with a smirk directed at Deanna.

"Do you reckon Talon could be quiet during sex?" I asked.

Okay. Maybe I was a tad intoxicated still because yelling was all I could manage.

"Jesus," Blue hissed.

"Talon owes us," Griz barked.

Julian ended up spitting his drink all over the table. Violet groaned and banged her head against the back of the booth. Pick asked for me to move so he could escape, and Deanna sat with her finger tapping her chin, pondering my question.

"Given his hotliness and badarseness, I highly doubt it," Deanna said. "Why the wondering?"

I sighed loudly. "I wanna have sex. I miss the pounding, the closeness, and the connection," I whined. "Hey!" I shouted, pointing at Griz and Blue. "No comment from the spunky men," I yelled before they could even think of commenting.

"Uh, Wildcat. Please, please move," Pick begged.

While continuing my rant, I moved and sat back down after Pick had escaped. "Six years, people. Six long years. Holy haemorrhoid, do you think my well's dried up?"

"Fuck me," Griz snapped.

"You don't want me to," Deanna supplied. I thought it had been quiet, but Griz turned a surprised stare upon her, which quickly morphed into a glare. Then he went back to looking at the crowd.

"You can't tell me—" Vi began.

"What?" Julian asked.

"Nope, I can't say it. That's my brother, for gonad's sake." She shuddered.

"Oh, oh! I think I know where you're going," Julian said, clapping. "And, cock ring, you can't deny the male fuckableness your bro is. Anyway, what she was getting at…you can't tell us that you and Spidey haven't done squat in the bedroom department."

I think I just blushed. Or the room had turned up twenty degrees.

"What the fuck, bitch? You have done something with the bossman and you ain't told me? Where's the friendship? I told you *all* about my last one not that long ago."

Griz flinched. Deanna smirked, but then quickly sent me her deadly glare. Thankfully, I was immune.

"Shit," Blue said. "I am not stayin' here to hear this crap. We can watch 'em from the bar." Blue stalked off, with Pick and a grumbling Griz not far behind.

"Maybe I should join them," Vi added. "I *really* don't feel like hearing about what my brother gets up to in bed. It'd probably cause me to chuck."

"Block your ears then," Deanna said.

I had to laugh when Violet did, in fact, block her ears.

"Quickly spill, muff lover," Julian cried, leaning forward over the table.

"There isn't much to say. As you can tell, we didn't do the deed…"

"But? Come on, woman, don't leave me hanging," Deanna said.

I blushed again. "I'm still kind of sensitive about it. Icameinliketwoseconds."

"Say what now?" Julian asked. "Sorry, dick sucker, I don't speak drunk-virgin-hymen-grown-over girl talk."

Groaning, I hid my eyes with my hand. "He went… you know… down yonder, and I was… um, done quickly."

"Did he care?" Deanna asked.

"No. Well, I don't think so, especially not when I reciprocated."

"Whoop, fuckin', whoop, girl. I'm so proud of you." Deanna beamed.

Deanna cheering me on made me smile. I should be proud; I was lucky I lasted that long after *six years,* and Talon didn't seem to have minded at all.

I got in closer and whispered, "He is huge."

"I hate you." Julian glared.

"You—"

"Hey there, sweetheart," a guy in his late forties said, as he stood at our table with two others. They all wore jeans and tees, with leather biker vests over the top. It was hazy, but I read the words 'Vicious Club' on the top patch.

The older one sat down beside me. "How's your night been, beautiful?"

I studied him for a second, and it was his eyes that told me he was harmless; the crinkle around them showing me he loved to laugh, and his smiling mouth told me he was caring. The thick salt-and-pepper hair told me my fingers wouldn't mind running through it to see if it was as soft as it looked.

His friends, though, were another story; they looked mean and scary. Which was why I leaned into him and whispered, "You seem like a nice guy, and I honestly mean it when I say that one day we could be friends, but —I'm sorry to say that your friends don't seem all that nice."

I sat back and watched him throw his head back and laugh a deep belly laugh.

"Oh, you are precious." He smiled.

"Which is why she's Hawks property," Griz growled from beside us where he stood next to Mean One and Mean Two.

Property, smoperty. I wasn't sure I liked that word yet.

Mr Nice looked up at Griz and asked, "Whose?"

"Talon's."

But I like that word.

"Wildcat, go and dance," Blue ordered.

Now he just popped up out of nowhere. I rolled my eyes and scooted around the other side, where Julian, Deanna, and Vi were already waiting for me.

Leaning over the table, I uttered, "It was nice meeting you…"

"Rocko," he supplied.

I smiled. "Rocko, and remember what I said." I got closer still. "I think you may need new friends."

"Thanks, sweetheart." He chuckled and then winked. "I'll keep that in mind."

Griz sat down as soon as I was out of the way. I moved off to the dance floor with my peeps to jiggle my flabby bits once again.

I was determined to have a great night.

We danced, we drank, and we sang our night into happiness.

Rocko and his mates had left probably an hour earlier, but I still couldn't fight the feeling of unease.

Then I thought it could be because I had to pee. Violet had gone to grab a drink, and while Deanna and Julian were being entertained by the Tina Turner wannabe, I went off in search of the toilet.

CHAPTER SIXTEEN

I woke up in the back of a strange car. My eyes were a little blurry, but once they cleared, I saw a gun pointed at my face. The guy who aim it was the one I'd seen walk into the girls' bathroom behind me at the bar, and he was also the one who had tasered me in the back after saying his boss wanted a word with me. It was just before I had the chance to scream.

"I don't know your boss," I croaked and sat up slowly.

My mouth was dry, and the great buzz I'd had going on at the club had disappeared, leaving me with a very nasty headache.

Though, that could also be from being *freaking* tasered.

"Yeah, well, he knows you, and when he wants something, he gets it." The guy smiled, showing crooked teeth.

If it weren't for those, he would have been an okay-looking man. He had a buzz cut, leaving dark-coloured fluff, and his eyes were brown. He had piercings in his lip, nose, and eyebrow, and seemed tall, slim and young. It was dark in and out of the car.

His companion who was driving was completely different. He had long dirty-blond hair; his build was larger, and he seemed shorter than Mr Talker.

I wondered if by now my friends knew I'd been kidnapped. I hoped they weren't panicking too much. My next thought was why wasn't I panicking? I felt a bit stressed, only relieved at the same time, because at least no one would get hurt when I was delivered to David. He'd already done many bad things to me; it couldn't get worse. Right?

I gulped.

At least Maya was safe.

The car suddenly stopped. It was then I realised I should have been taking in my surroundings to know where they were taking me in case of an escape. We'd pulled up outside of a huge house, one I didn't think was anything David would buy. It was old, yet beautiful. David loved new and exquisite things. My door opened. Mr Silent was there smirking in at me; he then jutted his chin out and up.

I stumbled out, and Mr Silent grabbed my arm, dragging me roughly forward and through the front door, down a hallway that took my breath away, and into a room that was a library. Books lined two walls from top to bottom. A large desk was in front of a huge bay window, where a man stood looking out. He turned with an intense gaze.

Oh. My. God. Where do they make these people? He was yet another good-looking older man, probably in his early forties, with dark hair and a few greys splattered at the sides. He had grey eyes and an athlete's form hidden behind a designer suit.

"Um, you're not David," I said, puzzled. What was I doing here and who was this guy?

"I hope my men weren't too forceful in getting you here."

"Do you call being tasered too forceful?" I asked with fake bravado, hands on my hips, glaring at him. On the inside I was chanting *I'm gonna die; I'm gonna die, and I never got to have sex with Talon.*

His fierce gaze turned to Mr Silent and Talker. "I told you to ask her politely. Did you even do that? Doesn't matter, get out of my sight," he snapped. "Please, Zara, have a seat, and I'm sorry for the way they treated you. It was not something I wanted."

Scepticism ran through my mind; still, I took a seat opposite him as he sat behind a large wooden mahogany desk that held papers scattered everywhere. "You have a nice home," I said. *Why am I being polite to the guy?* I cleared my throat. "Um, I mean, what am I doing here?"

"Thank you to the first." He smiled. "And to the second, I have some questions, to which I am sure you will have the answers."

"Sorry, but I doubt it. I don't know you." I looked down at my lap and adjusted my skirt.

"Pam, please come in," he called.

I turned in time to see the door open, and my jaw dropped. In walked the Pamela Anderson-wannabe from swimming that morning.

"You have got to be shitting me," I uttered. I watched her as she walked over to…heck, I didn't even know the guy's name, and stood beside him, smiling smugly.

"I can see that you recognise my girlfriend, Pam Knowles."

I snorted. I couldn't help it, and said, "Seriously, buddy, you need to find a new girlfriend."

He glared at me. "So what happened this morning was true? You verbally insulted and harmed Pam in front of my child."

I gasped.

"You see, Zara, I do not take kindly to this type of behaviour in front of my child, and I do not appreciate having my girlfriend mentally and physically hurt."

I slapped my hands on the desk and stood yelling, "Say what now? Look, buddy, I don't know who you are, and you seem like a nice sort of guy, but I can tell you now, I never did anything to your Pamela Anderson-wannabe."

"She's lying," Pam spat.

"Oh, my frigging God, are you really trying this on?" I glared and turned to her fella, offered an eye roll and added, "Buddy—"

"Travis Stewart," he supplied.

I sighed deeply. "Travis, I didn't even see a child with her. I only approached her because she was, and I'm sorry to tell you this, hitting on *my* man in front of *his* child. My man's son found me sitting down and he looked worried by it, so I got up to get rid of her. I may have called her a dog in heat, but other than that, I never did or said anything that was not appropriate." I raised my hands in the air and let them fall. "This is why I was tasered and brought here? Jesus, how bad is my luck right now? You know what? I really don't need this. I have enough going on." I flopped back in the chair.

"I'm sorry, Zara—"

"What are you apologising to her for?" Pam snapped.

Travis glared up at her. "Clearly, she is having a hard time in life right now." He stood to gaze down at her; she took a step back. "Tell me, Pam, is it true what you have told me, or is what Zara was saying true?"

"Travy, it wasn't like that. She's lying."

We all turned to the door when we heard a commotion outside of it. The door flew open, and in it stood Violet holding out her gun, pointing it inside the room.

"Travis?" She looked as though she knew him. She relaxed her form and stepped farther in.

I looked from Vi to Travis, and then back. Wait a cotton-pickin' minute. "That's *your* Travis?" I gasped. I turned back to Travis and appraised him in a new light.

"Violet. What are you doing here?" His tone held shock.

Vi shook her head and placed her gun away. *Hang on, should she be carrying a gun?* Because when I left, she was well on her way to being drunk. And where in the heck was Talon?

"I came for Zara." She walked over to stand beside me.

"Where are my men?"

Vi shrugged. "Unconscious. Travis, what's going on here? Why kidnap Zara?"

"Pam here told me Zara abused her in front of my child. I couldn't stand for that. I needed to have a word with her."

Vi scoffed. "Zara wouldn't hurt a fly." She jerked her head sideways to Pam. "She's lying."

"I am not," Pam screeched.

"Oh, just give up," I said to her, then to Travis, "Ask my man; he'll tell you."

"Travis," Vi said, catching his attention, "you *really* should have gone about this differenly."

"Why?"

"She's Hawks' property."

"Fuck," he hissed. "Whose?"

"Talon Marcus."

"Christ." He turned to Pam. Just from his look, I would have been scared as well. She was taking step after step away from him. "Get the fuck out of my house. You lied, and now I have this shit to fix. You're fuckin' lucky I don't kill you. You stupid bitch, in front of my baby, you whored yourself?" He ran a hand through his hair. "Leave. Now."

She ran from the room.

"Christ. Fuck!" Travis said as he paced the room, only to stop behind the desk again. "I am truly sorry for this, Zara." He looked at Violet. "When will I hear from Talon?"

"Not sure. He doesn't know yet."

Scoffing I asked, "How'd you pull that off?"

"I told the guys I'd be able to get you back before he found out. It was just lucky I saw those idiots leaving with you over one's shoulder. I followed and rang Griz on the way. He freaked. I told him I'd have you back soon, so we better get going."

"Wow, you're like a super-agent." I grinned.

"Yes." I watched Travis smile appreciatively, his gaze wandering up and down Vi's body. He turned back to me. "Please let me know if there is anything I can do for you.

Again, I am sorry for the way my men treated you, and for this…terrible misunderstanding. I'm sure I'll be hearing from Talon soon."

"Don't worry too much; it wasn't so bad, and I'll let Talon know that. I'm just thankful you know what a… nasty person your girlfriend is now. No one needs that around their child."

"That's true. You sound like you speak from experience."

I smiled. "I have a six-year-old daughter. It was just lucky I got away from my nasty before it could touch her."

"Zara, we better go," Vi said.

"Maybe one day, when we have more time, you could explain further on that topic?" Travis asked.

I cocked my head to the side. "You know what, maybe one day I will. And I'm sure Violet would love to come along as well."

He smirked, knowing full well that I knew about their past. "That would be wonderful. Coffee with two beautiful women."

"Alrighty, I'll be in touch. It was nice to meet you, Travis, and I'm glad it was you who kidnapped me." I smiled brightly and walked to the door with Violet following as she laughed.

Travis cleared his throat and said, "I had heard Talon had claimed an old lady. Now I can see why he has done it so quickly. I look forward to seeing you *both* soon. Please remember that if there is anything you need, call upon me."

"You may regret that," I said.

He chuckled.

We got outside to a vehicle that wasn't familiar to me. I looked at Violet, who was staring back, smiling. "Whose is this?" It certainly was a beauty.

We both got in before she answered, "Not sure. I had to find something quick to follow. But at least I'll be dropping it back, and hopefully, whoever this baby belongs to, they will be none the wiser." We both giggled.

What a frigging night.

ARRIVING BACK AT THE PUB, I could already see Griz, Pick, Deanna, Julian, and Blue standing outside waiting for us. As soon as we pulled up, my door was flung open, and I was pulled from the car by Blue, who examined my body for any signs of injury. Well, that was what I guessed he was doing when he ran his hands over me.

Deanna shoved him out of the way, saying, "You can cop a feel later. Bitch, what the fuck?" She grabbed me into a tight hug; a second later, Julian joined in.

"Guys, it's okay. It was *all* a misunderstanding. Travis didn't know his men were going to taser me—"

"You were fuckin' tasered?" Griz roared.

"Holy Mother Mary." Julian gasped, tears welling in his eyes.

"Arses. I'd like to have a chance at tasering them back," Deanna said with an evil look in her eyes as she rubbed her hands together.

"Shit, we need to tell Talon," Pick whispered. He looked worried.

"Don't worry, Pick. I'll explain it calmly and sweetly, and things will be fine," I reassured him.

Well, that was what I thought would happen. I didn't expect what did.

CHAPTER SEVENTEEN

Violet parked the car that she'd stolen back where it had been, and thankfully, no one was out looking for it. Vi ended up coming in Griz's car with us so we could drop her at home along the way. She sat between Julian and Deanna, as I was up the front with Griz that time. I think he was afraid to take his eyes off me in case something else happened and he'd then have to explain to Talon how he'd lost me a second time. Not that it would happen; my bad luck was done for the night… at least I hoped so.

On the way to Vi's, she explained a few things about good-old-rough-loving Travis. They'd met in university, both sharing a love of maths. They dated for a year, had mind-blowing sex—her words, not mine—but then he chose to move to Melbourne. He'd asked Violet to go with him; she said she wasn't ready for that. She loved the area and her family too much to leave it behind. He decided to go still; they visited and wrote for a while longer, but their lives eventually changed. They both became busy with their careers and drifted apart. I could tell it was something she had always regretted.

Travis was now a top-notch businessman. Well, he'd have to be to have security men working for him—who tasered people. I doubted I would ever get over that fact.

Travis also had that huge-arse house and expensive suit, which explained that he had money. So what had he been doing with a fluff-head like Pam instead of tracking down Violet? Someone had better talk with him. Of course, that someone had to be me. I smiled to myself and gave a mental pat on my back.

After dropping Vi off, we pulled up to the compound. I hadn't been watching where we were heading—again—so I wasn't expecting to be there. I just assumed Talon had left me to have a good night with the girls and had gone home to the kids.

Wow, that sounded fantastic in my head. *Gone home to the kids.*

So I was a little confused as to why Talon would still be here at one in the morning. And how had Griz known he was here?

Pick was ahead and he opened the door to the motorcycle clubhouse, a place I had never been inside before.

What I had expected, which was a run-down, dirty and smelly hole, was so different from what I saw. As we entered, there was a small hallway with a room on each side. The doors were closed, so I didn't get to see what was behind them. The hallway led us into… I supposed you could call it the main common room. It was large. Two massive tables and chairs were off to the left, and just behind them was a bar where three bikers sat whom I hadn't met. To the right of the room was a row of couches where they'd sit back, chill, and shoot the shit. Right in front of us, across the empty wooden floor, were another two long hallways and along them were many other doors.

"Right on. I need another drink," Deanna announced and dragged Julian along to the bar. Pick followed and greeted his other biker brothers with a handshake and then what you could call a man hug with a slap on the back.

"Yo, where's Talon?" Griz called.

The first one, an older man with grey hair and a long beard, scanned me from top to bottom with an approving look. Another biker looked down at the floor, and the last guy, who stood beside Pick, with long dark hair and wild dark eyes, gestured with his head to the long hallway across from us.

I was a little disappointed Talon wasn't out here to see

me, but then I had to remember he didn't know what had occurred as of yet.

No sooner had I felt that disappointment than it twisted into rage. A door at the end of one of the hallways caught my attention when I heard it click open. Out walked Talon with a woman clinging to the front of him as they hugged. Her back was facing me, and I watched as she looked up to my man, then Talon's head came down. It looked as if he was kissing her.

"Babe, not what you think," Blue whispered in my ear.

I call bullshit!

Enough! I'd had enough.

I found myself striding down the hall; some would have run the other way from a situation like that, but I was moving right into it. Talon must have heard my pounding feet approach, as he looked up with surprised eyes.

"Kitten, I—"

I wrapped my hand into the wench's hair and pulled her roughly back. She squawked in pain, and then I pushed hard, sending her crashing into the wall. A satisfied smile settled upon my lips.

"Kitten," Talon snapped.

"Don't you friggin' 'kitten' me, you arse. This,"—I pointed to the woman, who was leaning quietly against the wall while I yelled at arsehat—"this is what you've been doing while I was kidnapped and tasered?" I punched him in the stomach.

"That a girl," Deanna cheered.

"I should never have trusted you," I whispered. Tears filled my eyes. I went to punch him again for the hurt and betrayal I was feeling, but he caught my fist and pulled me closer to him, his eyes filled with fury.

He can suck his own dick. I am not sorry for punching him.

"You were kidnapped and tasered?" Talon's voice was a snarl.

Uh oh. I forgot calm and nice altogether.

"What the fuck, Zara?" His voice was a low outraged whisper.

"Everyone clear the room," Griz growled.

"Damn it, we're going to miss the fun again," Julian said.

"Call if you need me to kick his arse," Deanna yelled down the hall.

I didn't care. He didn't frighten me like David. He was pissed, but it wasn't at me. Well, not totally.

"Don't you 'what the frig' me, Talon Marcus, and get all alpha-angry. You don't get to be angry now! You didn't just walk in on me tonguing some guy."

"Hoo-wee. I like her," a deep voice said with a laugh.

"Colin, let's go," Blue said.

I heard some shuffling, and then doors being opened and closed.

Talon's grip gentled. "Babe, I just found out you were taken and tasered. Of course I'm gonna be pissed."

I got up close to him, nose-to-nose in fact, and snapped, "And I just found the guy I *was* with kissing some bimbo while all that went down. No, it's not the fact that you missed out on it all; it's the frigging fact that you had your tongue down someone else's throat!" I stepped closer again so our chests touched, and leaned my head back farther to keep eye contact. "There is no way you will ever get into my pants. I will deal with my stuff on my own. Now, I'm going to get Maya, and I don't want to see you again."

"Uh, sugar," the woman beside us said. I turned to glare at her. "It's not what you think, honey, we weren't kissing, and anyway, I'm—"

"Let's go into the office," Talon barked. He grabbed my wrist, spun and dragged me into the office with his tonguing friend, who closed the door behind us.

I pulled my arm free, went over to the far wall and sat on the dark blue couch with my arms crossed over my chest, glaring at them both. The room felt too small, having Talon and his hook-up in there with me, as well as two file cabinets that sat just behind the door. A desk had papers scattered all over it. *Someone needs to get organised.* Actually, the whole room needed a makeover; if felt gloomy. A few plants and a fresh coat of paint would do wonders.

Why am I thinking of decorating?

"Well?" I snapped. "I've got things to do. Hurry up and tell me your lies so I can be off."

"She's a feisty one, Tal. Perfect for you." Tonguer smiled as she perched her behind on the corner of the desk where Talon sat.

Good. Stay as far away as possible, arse.

"Zara, right?" she asked. I rolled my eyes. "I'm Livia. I manage Talon's strip club in Geelong."

"Oh, oh. How silly of me, so it was all a mistake. You were just here on a business date and they always end up with you two kissing each other." My voice dripped with sarcasm. I got up from the couch. "Now that we have all that settled, I'll see you guys around…like, say, never."

Livia grinned. "We weren't kissing. He's like a brother to me. We hug, talk close, but I promise you we weren't kissing."

"No." I shook my head. "I-I can't believe… it was too close, it looked… you were kissing." I was sure that was what I saw. "I-I knew you'd end up doing this to me." I closed my eyes, trying to control my emotions.

"Kitten." His tone was warm, soft.

"Zara," Livia said with a pleading tone. I opened my tired eyes. I just wanted to get Maya, go home and crash. "Honestly, for me, kissing Talon would have been gross."

Snorting, I shook my head and gave them a sad smile.

Did she really think I could believe that? I stood and started for the door.

"I'm gay."

Tumbling around fast, I tripped over my own feet and fell to the floor. With wide eyes, I watched Talon grin, and Livia, with a smile, walked over to me and helped me from the floor and back over to the couch, where she sat next to me.

She took my hand in both of hers and said, "I'm sorry that you thought you saw us in an embrace like that and it hurt you. I've known Talon for a long time, and I know he would never do anything on purpose to upset you in any way. He's like a brother to me, and *that* is all. Believe me when I say I'm 100% gay and I would rather have sex with you in a heartbeat than Talon any day."

I nodded numbly. She sounded like she was telling me the truth, but could I believe that?

"Livi, stop coming on to my woman," Talon said with an amused tone.

"Oh, shush. Tell you what, Zara, any time Talon and I have a business meeting, you can be there; and if you want, it can be you at the end who I hug."

"Christ. Livi, leave now before she thinks about letting you," Talon growled.

Livia giggled. "You're no fun, Tal." She kissed my hand, got up from the couch and went to the door. "Later, honey, and…" She winked. "I'll see you soon. Talon, now you have someone who'll make my visits worthwhile."

"Thanks." I winked back. "Oh, and sorry about being too rough with you before."

"That's all right. I enjoyed it."

"Jesus," Talon hissed.

Livia left laughing and shut the door behind her. The door I kept staring at because I didn't want to meet Talon's gaze. I could feel the heat of his stare, but I was embarrassed. Let's not forget tired from such a long, gruelling, and hard night.

"Kitten," Talon said softly.

"Yes?"

"Come here," he ordered.

"Nope, I'm all good here."

I heard his chair being pushed back. Excitement and worry coursed through my body as his footsteps approached. He sat next to me on the couch, and in the next second, I squealed, because I was pulled out of my spot and was straddling his waist. My skirt bunched up, and my exposed knees were around his hips. I looked at the roof with my arms crossed over my chest.

"Zara, look at me."

I shook my head. I could not look at him because I would cave. He looked and smelled too damn good.

"Kitten, please look at me."

"Why?"

"So I can tell you how fuckin' sorry I am. I wish you'd never seen that and I wish I could take the pained look I saw on your face, those tears that fell from your eyes, and wipe away any hurt you felt before you knew the truth." He reached behind my neck and pulled me closer so our foreheads touched and our eyes met. "It's you, kitten, ever since you rocked up to my door in a fuckin' nightie and combat boots. Now that I've finally gotten my arse into gear and claimed you, I'm never lettin' go. You are mine, kitten."

I breathed in a shuddering breath. "Does that mean you're mine?"

"In every way."

"No more… closeness with any other woman, even if they are gay."

He grinned. "No more, only and always just you."

CHAPTER EIGHTEEN

Our lips met in an urgent frenzy. I threaded my hands through his hair as he wrapped his arms tightly around my waist and pulled me closer. A moan escaped my lips. A deep growl left his, one I felt down to my toes.

I had never been kissed with such desire and passion.

Talon's hands fell from my waist and went to my thighs. Slowly and talentedly, he ran his hands up, sending a shiver throughout my body. I was already wearing an easy-access skirt, so I wasn't surprised when they dipped under and his thumbs gently rubbed my panty line.

Need surged through me, a need to rip our clothes away and have my wicked way with Talon once and for all.

He'd said he wanted to claim me by taking me; well I wanted the same. I wanted to claim everything about him so everyone knew he was mine and no one else's.

Especially if he kept up this teasing torture.

"Talon," I pleaded against his lips.

He smiled.

The arse.

His hands stilled, and then he whispered, "I won't have you here, kitten. Not in an office. You deserve a bed that I can lay you out on and fuck you until you scream my name over and over."

I rested my forehead against his shoulder and sighed. "No," I said, frustrated.

Talon chuckled. "What d'ya mean no, babe?"

Straightening, I crossed my arms over my chest and glared at him. "This is happening tonight and right frigging now."

"Kitten." His eyes warmed as he ran the back of his hand down my cheek.

"Talon. I mean it. We are going to have sex—" I leaned forward and hissed, "Now!"

"Jesus, babe, you're making this hard for me. I'm trying to be a fuckin' good guy here. You deserve care, time, and the right fuckin' place. I'm not takin' advantage of you."

"No, please advantage away on me, and you are a good guy, but if you don't do the dirty with me right now, you'll soon have a very pissed woman to deal with. We can take our sweet time another time and another place, with a bed and roses and songs. But right now, I want you to fuck me. Claim me."

His eyes flared, and from where I sat, something else flared in surprise. On a growl, he lifted me in his arms and off the couch. I wrapped my legs around his waist as he carried me to the desk where, with one hand, he swept all papers, the phone, and junk onto the floor to sit my butt on the edge.

"You want me to fuck you, I will. Really, I'm more than happy to, but next time we do it, we're gonna take our time so I can cherish every fuckin' part of your sweet body."

I gulped, nodded, and grinned like a fool. "I'm up for that, honey."

He closed his eyes and whispered, "Christ, I love hearing you call me that, kitten." Upon opening his eyes, he reached between my legs, which were still wrapped around his waist. He moved back, so they dropped, and he slowly pulled my underwear down and threw them away. "I'd love to taste you right now, babe, but my woman wants me to fuck her, so that's what I'm gonna do."

"Yippee," I cheered.

Talon laughed, shook his head, and his eyes turned serious. I watched him, and could have dribbled as he popped the button on his jeans and slowly slid the zipper down.

"Jesus, kitten, you turn me the fuck on just from the way you watch me." He licked his lips. "Are you ready for me, babe? Are you wet for me?" He ran a finger through my folds to see that, yes indeed, I was wet, ready and waiting. I shivered as I watched him raise that finger, place it in his mouth, and suck my juices off, causing a moan from Talon and a groan from me.

"Fuckin' beautiful," he hissed, and then surged his hips forward. In one quick swoop, he was bedded deep inside of me.

"Oh, God," I moaned. My head tipped back and my chest arched forward. I was in heaven. *Happy birthday to me; happy birthday, and Christmas, and all the other holidays, to me.*

"No, kitten, not God, just your man." Talon smiled. I swivelled my hips and that smile fell from his face. He pulled out slowly and plunged back in. "Goddamn, kitten, you're so fuckin' tight and wet."

After that comment, all hell broke loose. I grabbed Talon by the shoulders and pulled him forward so our lips met. As we kissed and bit, Talon pumped me hard and good, just the way I wanted it.

It was possible I would not be walking tomorrow, and at that point I did not care.

"Talon, oh, God, Talon." I groaned. It was building and it was a big one.

"Let it go, babe," Talon growled at my neck.

"Talon."

"Let it go."

"H-honey." I arched as my climax crashed over me, and I was sure I was going to black out. But I made myself focus and opened my eyes to see Talon still over and in me, pumping hard and watching me with hooded eyes. One, two, three pumps later, he groaned, swore, and collapsed on top of me.

"You're gonna fuckin' kill me, babe, but it'll be worth it." He pulled back to look at me, smiling. "So hot, so wet, so tight. Never had it like that before, babe. You're so fuckin' responsive; I'm never gonna wanna leave you or your pussy again."

I giggled. "That's okay, 'cause me or my…yeah, are never going to want you to leave."

I liked the way his eyes shone with more desire for me, until they turned teasing. "I fucked you hard, you screamed my name, and you still can't say pussy? Babe."

"Shud'up and kiss me."

He grinned and obliged.

"You need to get cleaned up, kitten. We got shit to talk about, once a-fuckin-gain, then we gotta get home to the kids."

I rolled my eyes, but did a happy dance on the inside,

and then shoved him out of the way. "Yes, Talon." I moved off to the door, picking up my underwear along the way.

"Well, shit, babe. If all I gotta do is fuck you for you to be obedient, then be prepared to be on your back all the goddamn time."

"Whatever," I snapped. But smiled.

"Kitten—"

"Talon, honey. You want me to get cleaned so we can talk or what?"

"Bathroom's right across the hall." He smirked.

"I knew that." Although I hadn't, but he didn't need to know.

AFTER I CLEANED UP, went back in the office and had a make-out session with Talon, he informed me one of his men had dropped Julian back at his house. Then he told me that Deanna had gone to bed in Griz's room, as he dragged me down the hall past the main room I'd walked into when we arrived, which was now empty, and into what Talon called 'the meeting room'. It was just as big as the main room. Two large tables sat in the middle, wooden kitchen chairs piled around it, and they were mostly filled with bikers. A bar—of course, another one—was at the back of the room. Some old arcade games and a ping-pong table—yes, apparently bikers played table tennis, giggle—sat at the other end of the room.

As soon as we'd entered, and the bikers noticed us, they started clapping, cheering and swearing. One cheer caught my attention, "Christ, 'bout time you claimed all of her."

Holy shit.

Had they heard?

I knew my cheeks were flaming red, and I gripped Talon's hand tightly.

"H-how?" I whispered to Talon, but apparently I hadn't said it low enough because it was Blue who answered.

"Baby, Talon wouldn't walk in 'ere with a smile on his face after findin' out you'd been kidnapped. And you just confirmed what we guessed was happening."

I was more than embarrassed; I was annoyed and pissed. "Oh. My. God. Shut up. Seriously? Right, from now on, no one talks about me and Talon in front of me and Talon—unless, that is, Talon wants guy time and I've pissed him off in some way and he needs to vent. But that's it. We do not—" I turned to Talon, glaring. "—talk about our private time to anyone. Well, except for me, of course. I mean, come on, that's a given; I'm a woman and we talk about this stuff…I think *I'll* shut up now." I crossed my arms over my chest, stalked to the table and plopped down in the chair at the end while the room erupted in laughter.

"Shhhit, brother, where can I get me one of her?" someone asked.

Talon, grinning like a fool, walked over, pulled me out of my chair, sat down, and then tugged me down onto his lap. I tried to move, but he wouldn't have it.

"She's one of a kind, and what she says goes. No one is to embarrass her like that again. 'Less you want to hear her rant once more." Talon chuckled as I jabbed him in his side with my elbow.

Seconds later, all joking left Talon's body. He stiffened, and eyeing Blue, Griz, and Pick he asked, "Right, who wants to start with why the fuck my woman was tasered, taken, and got free without me knowing about it?"

The whole room took on a tenser atmosphere, as if Talon was a lion and they were waiting for him to attack. Maybe that 'Talon and Zara happy fun time' hadn't sedated his pissed-off-ness.

"Honey, can't this wait till morning? I'm tired and I'm sure all the fellas are as well. It's been a long night. Can't we just go home?"

"No, kitten."

I rolled my eyes, sighed, and looked heavenward.

"Well, don't blame me if I pass out from exhaustion

and hit my head on the table, get a concussion and then have to go to hospital."

"Babe." Talon smiled when I looked down at him. "I'd catch ya. Your head would never touch the table."

Oh, wasn't that sweet, but he was totally missing the point. I needed a bed and now.

"I'm spent. Being kidnapped, tasered, witnessing you tongue-bathing another woman, fighting, yelling, and mind-blowing sex can do that to a person."

Hands slapping the table, laughter, chuckling and shouting made me realise I had just said *that* aloud.

Holy crab cake.

With wide eyes, I looked down at Talon's satisfied face and uttered, "I said that out loud."

"Yep." He nodded, his eyes laughing.

"See?" I whined. "I'm tired. I need sleep, honey, and now. Plus, I want the kids to wake up with a parent home."

"All right, babe."

I grinned. "We're going home?" I asked as the bikers around the table talked and joked amongst themselves.

"You are. I need to find out what happened. I can't have anyone think they can do that shit to my woman without payback —"

"Talon, please. It was a mistake. Don't do anything to Travis—"

"I might just visit him, kitten. But if I don't like what he says, then we're gonna have problems."

"There won't be a problem. He's nice. He's got a daughter, and we're going to catch up for coffee one day—"

"What the fuck, babe?"

I sighed. "Don't worry, honey…hey, that rhymes—worry-honey." I giggled to myself. God, I was way over-tired. "Anyway, you don't have to worry. He's got a thing for Violet, and a history. So she'll be coming with me when we catch up, a-a-and, if you want to work things out with your sister, it may be good not to *off* the guy she likes."

Talon shook his smiling face. "You make friends wherever you go, even after the guy fuckin' kidnaps you. Babe, get your arse home for that sleep before the kids wake up." He looked over my shoulder. "Pick, take Zara to my house."

"Sure, boss," Pick said, standing from the table, suddenly looking gloomy.

"Kitten, I need your mouth before you go. And don't worry, I won't off the guy."

"Thanks, honey." I grinned and kissed my man.

CHAPTER NINETEEN

Pick drove for a long, silent, fifteen minutes. He seemed to have something on his mind and any other time, I would have asked about it to see if I could be of some help, but I was beat. We pulled onto a dirt driveway that wound around to a massive ranch-style home. It was the prettiest white weatherboard house I had ever seen, with a large deck surrounding it.

"Wildcat, wait here a sec before we go in. I need to make a call." Without an answer, he climbed out of the car, shut the door, flipped his phone open, and placed it to his ear. I couldn't make out what was being said. He was speaking in a hushed tone, but whatever it was, Pick didn't seem happy about it at all. He waved his free arm wildly in the air, trying to get some message across that, obviously, someone wasn't getting.

I turned my attention back to the house. Most lights were off except the porch, and what I presumed would be the lounge. How had Talon afforded a place like this? It looked as though—from what I could see in the dark—along with the house, there was some mighty big acreage going on.

"Fuck," I heard yelled, bringing my gaze back to Pick just as he pounded the bonnet with his fist. He swung the door open and snapped, "Let's move."

Undoing my belt, I got out and met him at the front of the car. "Pick, are you okay?"

He grabbed my upper left arm and pulled me toward the house. "No, Wildcat, I'm not. I hate my fuckin' life right now. All I ever do is try to protect my ma, but she just keeps bringin' shit into her life, and then I have to fuckin' fix it. It sucks." We stopped just outside the front door as he turned me to face him. "Shit, Zee, sorry."

"Don't worry about it. You need to talk to get it off your chest, and maybe when I'm not so dog-tired, I could have some great advice for you, but right now, I doubt anything that came out of my mouth would be understandable."

He hunched and looked to his feet. "You're a great person, Wildcat…and, I'm sorry—"

What?

The front door opened to a smiling Vic. "Come on in, sweet stuff." He reached out and grabbed my hand, dragging me forward, but I couldn't move my gaze from Pick. He seemed truly worried and remorseful. His eyes moved from the floor to me rapidly.

Finally, he met my stare and whispered, "I would never have done this if it weren't for me protecting my ma. Never. I'm sorry."

Shaking my head, I smiled. "Pick, what are you talking about?"

"Momma."

I spun so fast I would have fallen if Vic still didn't have hold of my hand. "Maya—" It was then I took in the scene in front of me, and I felt sick to my stomach. "W-what's going on?" I asked with wide eyes, staring at Julian and Mattie sitting on the floor near the far wall, cradling a scared Maya and Cody. I turned to Vic and noticed for the first time he held a gun.

"Have you worked it out yet?" He smirked.

"Not really," I hissed, ripping my hand from his grip. "But please, enlighten my tired brain."

He chuckled. "I can see why Talon likes you, showing balls in the face of danger. Please, have a seat while we wait." He shoved me to the couch near my family.

Straightening my clothes and myself, I looked over to the children. "It's going to be fine, okay?"

"Yes, Momma," my brave Maya said. Cody nodded.

Looking back at Vic and Pick—yes, any other time I would have laughed at the rhyming; instead I said, "I can sort of understand your reason, Pick. But, Vic, why?"

He shrugged. "I need the money."

"What's he paying you to deliver me?"

"Smart girl."

I shrugged. "Doesn't take a genius to work it out."

"I guess not. Between the four of us, we get fifty thousand each. Easy money really. All we have to do is keep you here till the delivery guys arrive. Easy as pie."

"Do you really think you'll get the money in the end?" I studied him. "Oh, my God, you do. Well, I guess you're as stupid as *you* look." I laughed, until he wiped that laugh from my face by slapping me. My head jerked to the side. Maya screamed. Mattie swore. "It's okay. I'm okay," I reassured them.

"He will pay or he knows I'll come after him," Vic screamed.

"Chill, man," Pick said.

"You fuckin' chill. I'm not the one chickenin' out. Now everyone shut the fuck up." He glared at me and took a step closer to say, "I may have to deliver you and the kids, but it doesn't have to be in one piece."

I gasped. "Kids? No, please no. Leave them here, please."

Vic chuckled a sardonic laugh. "I don't think so. At least then I'll know you'll behave for their safety. Not only for them, but if you try shit on the delivery, I'll kill your brother and his…" he looked at Julian in disgust, "…thing."

Jesus. What the hell am I going to do?

"W-why Cody too?"

"To shove it up Talon. Thinks he's hot shit. I'll show him."

"And you're okay with this, Pick?" I asked, tears threatening.

"No." He shook his head, again looking at his feet. "But if I don't get that money, my ma will be killed by loan sharks."

"Talon would have helped you. Why didn't you go to him?"

"I couldn't. I was…ashamed."

"And you thought this was the best way out of that black hole? To ruin other people's lives? Especially one who took you in, who looked out for you."

"Shut up, bitch," Vic snapped, hitting me in the back of the head.

"Vic, don't," Pick growled.

"Don't get a conscience now. Man up, fucker."

"God, please, please, just let the kids leave with Mattie and Julian. Please, I won't cause any trouble; I promise. I won't do anything; just let them go."

"Zara, it's no use," Mattie said. I turned my wet eyes upon them.

Regret.

All I could feel was regret, because they were here because of me. *I'm sorry,* I mouthed. I watched Julian's bottom lip tremble as he gripped Maya closer, and Mattie shook his head at me with a sad smile on his mouth.

"W-where are t-the others who came here? Didn't you get dropped off, Julian?"

Vic laughed. "Still holding out for someone to save you? Won't happen tonight. Your man will be very busy with the planned distraction."

"What?" I hissed, through clenched teeth.

"Yeah, I saw that bitch at the pool all over Talon. She didn't like to be dissed as nothing. So I approached her, asked her to help me out a bit. She went home crying to her fella. I rang her and told her where you'd be...after my man Pick had informed me. She mentioned it to her man, and he sent his guys to pick you up. Didn't think it'd be that easy, but you were stupid enough to go to the crapper on your own. So now, Talon will keep himself busy defending his woman, and while that's happening"—he laughed—"his life will be shattered right from under him."

The room fell silent.

All I could think about was scratching out his eyes. How dare he do this to Talon, to Cody and Maya?

Julian cleared his throat. "I was dropped off out the front, pumpkin. Walked in here blind to the trouble, just like you did."

"The other guys left when"—Mattie pointed at Pick—"he called them and told them it was fine to cut the guarding down to one. Vic offered to stay."

Shit. They had it all worked out.

I wanted to crawl up in a protective ball and cry, but then again, I wanted to rip their dicks off and slap them over their heads with them.

Oh, God. Talon.

He was going to go crazy, especially when he found out I'd dragged his son, his only boy, into this mess. He'd be on a warpath, and anything that crossed it was going to be destroyed.

I didn't even get to tell him I loved him.

Love him?

Yes.

Because I did.

Sure, to start with it was lust at first sight. But the care, the gentleness and protectiveness he had shown me…not only me, but Maya, and even Deanna, Mattie and Julian, had my heart beating in love for the first time in seven years.

All I could do now was suck up all my emotions and feelings, and stay sane and safe for the children. They were what mattered now.

What a fuckin' well-planned night.

I was just about ready to see my ex and punch him in the gonads for this.

I shook my hands out and rubbed my eyes. I was beyond tired, but I had to stay focused for the kids.

What about Mattie and Julian?

Yes, what was going to happen to them once we left? I looked over to my beautiful brother and brother-in-law. I wouldn't be able to handle it if something did happen, but I really didn't like our chances.

"It's okay, sis." Mattie smiled. Had he read the anguish in my eyes?

We all turned to the sound of a vehicle coming up Talon's dirt driveway.

"They're here," Vic said. He went to the window, looked out, and then walked out the front door to greet them, leaving Pick behind.

Duh. I had felt like saying, sarcasm was something I hid my fear behind, but now wasn't the time for it.

"Come on, poppet. Go to your mum," Julian said as he helped Maya stand on shaky legs. She hugged and kissed them both, whispering something in their ears, causing them both to pull their lips between their teeth. Maya then ran to me and climbed onto my lap, her tiny arms encircled my neck.

Mattie coughed to clear his throat. "Up you get, too, Cody," Mattie ordered. Cody mumbled something to them and they nodded.

Shit, shit, shit. I couldn't do this. I couldn't leave my brothers. I closed my eyes to fight the tears.

"Zee, honey." I opened them to Mattie. He ushered Cody forward, and Cody came to sit at my side. I placed my arm tightly around his shoulders while I held Maya just as tightly as I could with the other.

Looking back at Mattie and Julian, I forced a smile. "I love you, g-guys." I bit my bottom lip for control.

Mattie shuffled closer to a crying Julian and placed his arms around him. "We love you, too, sis. And we wouldn't change anything. We still would have come. We still would have stayed because it meant we got to spend more time with you. You, who I have missed for six years."

I closed my eyes and nodded, leaning my head against Maya's as she hid her face in my shoulder. I wasn't surprised that she hadn't cried. When she was under stress, like I had witnessed when she went to her first swimming lesson, she turned quiet. Her fear built inside her, and the only way she really showed it was through her body. She was shaking like a leaf in the wind. Just for that, and the fact that Cody showed his fear by being a silent statue, his form as stiff as a board, it made me want to buy myself a machine gun and shoot Vic while he tried to run for his life.

Though, I knew I wouldn't have it in me to harm Pick. I could tell that he honestly would not be involved in any of this if it wasn't to save his mother. Anyone could see that he knew this was the wrong choice. He was the one who was going to have to live with this regret…and that was only if Talon didn't get to him first.

Still, it also showed me that Pick was loyal. But in my opinion, he was being loyal to the wrong person. Yes, it was his mother, but a mother should never have dragged her own child into her mess. A mother was there to protect and provide for her child…not the other way around.

I felt for Pick, because in one way or another, he was going to be living his own personal hell.

Of course, I wouldn't allow myself to feel too deeply for him, because if he hadn't played a part in all this, I doubted I'd be in this situation.

Julian cleared his throat and clapped. "Enough of this crap. Honey, do not worry; we'll be fine, and you'll all be fine. Cody's superhero daddy will come to the rescue. Won't he, mate?"

"He will." Cody nodded with confidence.

I gave him a squeeze. He looked up at me and I winked. The front door opened and my mouth dropped open when Rocko's men, the ones I had seen at the bar, walked in.

I knew it.

I frigging knew it.

They were trouble, nothing but trouble.

More men added to the list I'd gun down in the bloodbath I was willing to orchestrate.

But how did they know about this? About me and David?

"Get up, bitch," Vic snapped. I placed Maya to stand on the floor beside me, and stood from the couch, pulling Cody up with me. I wrapped my arms around each child.

"We'll come, nothing will happen. We won't do anything...just, just don't hurt my brother and Julian."

"Yeah, we'll see." The glint in Vic's eyes sent dread to the pit of my stomach. "Keep me posted," Vic said to the two men. They gave him a chin lift in return.

I turned to Julian and Mattie. "I'll see you soon, yeah. Okay?"

"Of course you will, cupcake." Julian smiled.

"Be smart and safe, sis," Mattie uttered.

I nodded, because I knew if I spoke, I'd break down. Instead, I mouthed, *I love you both.* And even that caused tears to fill my eyes. I choked back a sob and pulled the kids in tighter.

With one man in front of us, and one behind, I followed them out to a black SUV. The man in front opened the door and we were pushed inside. The men got in and the scarier one with a scar running through his upper lip turned in his seat and threw something that landed in my lap.

"Put them on. All of you."

I moved my arm from around Cody and picked up the pieces of fabric. They were head sacks.

CHAPTER TWENTY

PICK

W*hat the fuck have I done?* The front door closed behind Wildcat and I wanted to run out, shoot the motherfuckers, and save the day. But I couldn't, or my own ma would be dead by tomorrow. I needed this money. *This last time.*

No matter how much it had hurt to watch the dicks take them.

Fuck.

I'd never forget the look on Cody's face when I walked in and did nothing to help the situation. I let Vic hit Wildcat. I just stood by and did nothing…like the pussy I was.

I was scared, and that was all it came down to.

And it fuckin' hurt.

It hurt to see the pain in Wildcat's eyes. She felt betrayed by me, and it was justified.

Vic raised his gun and pointed it at the gay guys. "Right, change of plans. I have to get out of here now, so we gotta kill these fuckers."

I stepped forward, hands raised. "What? No way, man. That wasn't the plan. We need to stick to the plan."

"Can't. They can't live. You should'a figured that out from the start, brother. They know us and they'll run to Talon. Then, we're as good as dead."

"Please, no," Julian cried. Mattie stared at us with wide eyes. But his eyes also showed that he hadn't expected anything different to come from us. He closed his eyes as he pulled Julian closer, and rested Julian's forehead against his shoulder.

I felt disgusted in myself.

Fuck!

I couldn't let this happen. I would not have more blood on my hands. The only reason I let Wildcat go was because I knew her dickhead ex wouldn't kill her.

Yeah, you just keep tellin' yourself that.

I had to believe that. Or else I did all this for nothing. Really, I did it for nothing anyway. I already knew my ma wouldn't change, and it made me feel sick. Give her six months and she'd be back to owing, in more ways than one.

So why was I helping her now? After what she'd done? After the hell she'd put me through all my fuckin' fucked-up life. Who did that to their child?

Who sold their own child's body to be used by rich fat-arse bitches?

Jesus.

I couldn't let this happen.

"No, Vic."

He turned his hard stare on me, but I gave as good as I got and met his gaze with my own.

"What the fuck you mean, no?"

"This ain't happenin'." I pulled out my own gun from where it sat at the back of my pants at my waist, and pointed it at Vic. He didn't think I had it in me. That I'd shoot. I could tell, because he still held his gun at the gay guys.

"Don't do this, brother. Don't fuck this up for the both of us just 'cause you're a pussy and can't kill two fuckin' poofs."

"I should never have been involved. I should have manned up at the start and told Talon your plan, but I didn't, and I let Wildcat walk out. Christ, with her kids, and I'm gonna have to live with that. But I can't let you do this. I won't let you kill them."

One of them gasped, but I didn't dare look their way.

"You're pathetic. Why Talon ever let you join, I'll never fuckin' know. You could never handle the paybacks for the club. You're useless."

Scoffing to myself, I thought, *I guess he'll soon find out how useless I am.*

I watched his hand twitch and I knew.

I knew I was about to be shot.

But I had to get there first.

The sound of my gun being fired echoed through the quiet house.

Though, it wasn't only my gun.

I was knocked back when I was hit. My hand went to my chest as I stumbled backwards and then fell to my arse against the wall.

I smiled as I witnessed Vic fall to the floor, bleeding out from his throat.

We all watched silently as he took his last staggering breath and died.

"Holy shit," Mattie yelled.

"Mother Mary," Julian cried.

I snorted, and then winced from the pain. My hand was still holding my chest as the blood seeped through my fingers.

"G-get to Talon. Tell him," I said.

"We aren't leaving you," Julian uttered as he knelt down beside me. Mattie showed up with a towel in his hand, gave it to Julian, and then he disappeared again with a phone to his ear. I watched in slow motion as Julian moved my hand away and placed the towel and pressed against my chest, causing me to moan as the pain doubled.

"Right, there's an ambulance on the way."

"No," I whispered.

I was better off dead.

"Don't shit us. You're going to the hospital and that's final," Mattie ordered, and he knelt down on my other side, moved Julian's hand away and placed his in the spot. "You saved us. We save you."

I snorted again, but it turned into a cough. "N-no mouth-to-mouth."

They laughed a tired, stressed laugh. "You wish," Julian said.

"Handsome," Mattie said—I hoped to fuck to Julian. I glanced up and saw he was staring at his lover. "You need to go to Talon. Call Violet on the way; she'll need to be there. I'll stay here. We'll meet up later."

Julian shook his head. "I'm not leaving you. We can call him."

"No. We can't tell him this over the phone. Listen, here comes the ambulance. Go, Julian. Do this for Zee."

Yeah, finding out his brother betrayed him wasn't something to say over the phone.

Julian kissed Mattie quickly—not something a dying

man wished to see. He got up and ran out the front door, yelling to the ambo guys on the way, "It's not my blood; in the house, get in the house."

CHAPTER TWENTY-ONE

TALON

I'd just pulled up to the compound from visiting Travis when Pick's car came burling around the corner and skidded to a stop beside Griz and me. Only it wasn't Pick who got out, but Julian. Covered in blood.

My stomach dropped.

Pain filled my chest.

"What the fuck?" I roared.

"Inside now," Griz ordered to a pale-faced Julian. We ran. Julian ran straight for the bar; with shaking hands, he poured himself a shot and downed it.

I stalked over to him and yelled, "Tell me what the fuck is going on."

"Oh, God, Talon, shit, shit."

"Talk now, motherfucker, or so help me—where the fuck is my woman…fuck, the kids?"

"Brother, calm down," Griz said.

"Fuck!" I screamed.

"What the hell is going on?" Deanna asked, walking into the room in shorts and a tee that she'd slept in. Her mouth dropped open at the sight of Julian. "No." she gasped.

Griz went to her, pulling her into his arms; she shoved him away and with her hands on her hips and cold eyes she asked, "What happened?"

"Vic," Julian said.

"What the fuck about Vic?" I asked as I started pacing. It was either that or I'd lose my fuckin' mind.

"H-he's got men delivering Zara and the kids to David right now."

I picked up a chair and threw it against the wall, shattering it.

"Where's Pick, Stake, and Bizz?" Griz asked.

"Shit, Talon. I'm sorry, man. Pick had called your house, even before I got there, and told them they didn't need to guard anymore. Bizz and Stake left it in the hands of Vic. Zee got back with Pick…shit. They had it all planned. Even tonight, the distraction of Travis—not that he knew, but his slutty girlfriend helped Vic set it up."

"Christ," I said to the roof. "My brothers betrayed me."

"Yeah," Julian whispered. "But then, Vic was going to kill Mattie and me once the others left with Zara—the others being Rocko's men, the ones we saw tonight."

"Motherfucker," I roared.

"How'd you get away?" Deanna asked as she stood there with her arms wrapped around her stomach. I knew she'd be feeling just as sick as I was.

Only hatred and fury filled me more, and I was willing to ride those fuckin' emotions to lead me to my woman, my son, and my Maya.

"Pick. H-he, God, he helped us. He didn't want to do this Talon. He hated every moment. But he's got some mother issues. He s-shot Vic, but got shot in return. Mattie's with him. They're going to the hospital."

"And Vic?" Griz hissed.

"He's dead."

"At least that's one less arsehole we'll have to kill," I said. "Right, Julian, go get cleaned up; I'll send someone down with clothes for you. Then get to the hospital with one of my guys to be with Mattie. No one takes their eyes off Pick. I'll need a word with him."

The door to the compound burst open, and in ran Violet, Warden, and Travis.

"What's going on?" Vi asked when she came to stop beside me.

"In short, I was betrayed by two of my brothers; Zara and the kids have been taken to David."

"Fuck," Warden whispered.

"Christ, no," Vi uttered.

"What can we do?" Travis asked. Any other time I would have told him to fuck off, but not when my family was involved.

Only nothing came to mind. All I could think about was hurting someone. I needed someone to pay for the gaping hole I was feeling in my heart.

Thank fuck I had Griz at my side. He barked out, "Violet, you stay here with Deanna and man the phones. Travis, see if you can find out where David is situated right now through your sources. Warden, you'll go with Blue. Once I call him in to the hospital, you'll need to talk to Pick. Talon…"

I smiled. "We're going to talk to Rocko."

Travis got on his phone. Griz got on his to call Blue. Julian took off to the showers; but it was Deanna and Violet both at the same time who yelled, "Fuck no."

Then Deanna added, "You can't expect me to sit on my arse while my best friend is out there having God-knows-what done to her by that fucker David. I'm not sitting here manning the fuckin' phones when you can get some of your boys to do it."

"I agree." Vi voiced. "You need me, Talon. We don't see eye-to-eye on a lot of things, but this, we work together on."

"Fuck, woman. I don't need this shit. I gotta go."

"Then we're coming with you," Violet said.

"Shit yeah," Deanna added.

"Jesus, whatever. Griz?"

"Jeremy's up. He'll call others to scout, and man the fuckin' phone. Let's roll."

A curt nod and we left.

Not fuckin' before I saw Travis—the biggest pimp in Melbourne—pull my sister aside, kiss her, and tell her something to have her eyes warm and nod.

Fuck, it was something to worry about when I got my family back.

Now it was time to fight for them.

CHAPTER TWENTY-TWO

ZARA

All I knew was that we drove for a very long time. Long enough that the kids fell asleep in my arms, leaning their heavy weight upon me, and it was long enough for me to doze off and on for quite some time.

I think my relaxed state showed the children not to worry, and in turn they weren't, so they could sleep knowing that I'd be there to protect them.

There were many reasons why I was relaxed. For one, alcohol still flowed through my body, and two, I knew Talon would go to great lengths to find us, and finally three, I was stronger in mind, body, and spirit to deal with an arsehat like David.

The only thing that had me worried, but I didn't let show, was how all this was going to be played out. What was David going to do? At least I was sure he would never harm a child. I—on the other hand—was a different story altogether. Though, I wasn't worried for myself, only and always for the children.

So to keep my relaxed state for the kids, I thought of Talon.

His eyes and how they grew soft for me.

His mouth when he smiled at me.

His hands and body, and how he always sought me out in a room.

Him.

The perfect, dominating, alpha bossy biker, who was a hard-scary-arse, beautifully hot, delicious man.

Sometimes, I had to focus, because my mind kept supplying me with other freaked-out thoughts of *Mattie, Julian, Mattie, Julian. God, I hope they're okay. I have to be good. I cannot rip into these guys like a momma T-Rex because...Mattie, Julian, Mattie, Julian.*

However many seconds, minutes, or hours later, the car came to a stop. The kids were roused from their sleep, and again, I reassured them that things were going to be okay.

"Keep the masks on," one of the men ordered. The doors opened and we were pulled out onto a gravel road. I took Cody and Maya's hands, and our feet crunched the gravel under us as we stumbled blindly along. A door was opened. Thankfully, there were no steps or I would have fallen flat on my face, bringing the children down with me.

"It's going to be okay," I said for the umpteenth time, and received a hand squeeze from both.

We were placed in a room in front of—I guessed—a couch, which I felt at the back of my calves.

"Sit," one kidnapper said. We sat, and I cradled the children close to me. The door opened again. Someone walked in and I heard a chair being slid back, the sound of *that* someone sitting in it. I knew who it was straight away. I could never misplace his strong, stinking cologne.

"Remove," David said, with a smile upon his mouth. I'd been around him enough to know when he was smiling.

Our head covers were whipped off. I blinked a couple of times to bring focus back. The kids rubbed at their eyes. I looked up and found David sitting behind a desk, his hands folded on top of it; his eyes gleamed with a 'gotcha' look, and his mouth was smirking at me. He looked the same as he had six years ago. The same ocean-blue eyes that had sucked me in, the same slim, tall form. The only difference was that his sandy hair had receded more on top.

"Hello, my dear Zara *Edgingway*." he gleamed.

"David."

"What, that's it? That's all you have to say to your husband? After all these years," he spat, disgusted. "Get the kids out of here. I want to talk to my wife."

"What? No, no, David. Please let them stay with me," I begged. I didn't trust the men standing behind the couch. Especially the one looking eagerly at my daughter.

David chuckled. "I doubt they'd want to hear what we have to talk about, darling."

"You leave her alone," Cody yelled as he stood from the couch.

"Cody," I said, pulling him back beside me. "It's okay, hun." I kissed the top of his head and looked at David again. "David, do you at least have someone who could be trusted with them? Please."

He did a full belly laugh. "Of course I do." He picked up the phone, pushed a button, and said into it, "Bring them in."

Moments later, the door opened and a guy in jeans and a long-sleeved black tee walked in. But I was more interested in the voice I heard in the hall.

"Are you bastards ever going to let us go? You know I've missed my tit appointment; not that I'd really want to get them squished into a vice, but it has to be done with a woman my age. Plus, my kids must be worried by now."

A sigh. "Nancy." And I knew that person would be shaking his head.

"Mum?" I called, shocked.

I stood as an older version of me walked into the room, wearing black pants and a red woollen jumper. Behind her was a brooding form of an older version of Mattie, only he was taller, with dark grey hair and warm, green eyes. Both of them looked a little worse for wear; there was a bruise on Mum's cheek and Dad had a black eye.

I felt sick.

David was going to pay.

"Dad?"

"Oh, my baby," Mum cried, and she ran at me.

"Mum, oh, God, Mum, Dad," I sobbed.

"Sweetheart," Dad said with tears in his eyes. They both wrapped me up in their arms.

"Oh, oh, is this my little angel, Maya?" Mum pulled away, picked Maya up, and hugged her to her chest.

"And who do we have here?" Dad asked. "Hey, buddy. I'm Richard, Zara's dad, and that loud lady is Nancy, Zara's crazy mum."

"I heard that, Richard, and I'm not crazy."

"It's so great to see you both," I cried. "A-and this is Cody. Talon's son."

"Really, and who's Talon?" Mum asked.

"He's my mum's man, Nanny," Maya informed.

"My dad's the one who's gonna come here and kick his arse," Cody whispered to my parents. I pulled him into a hug.

"Well, we look forward to meeting him."

David cleared his throat. "As do I. Now, isn't this reunion grand? But it ends now."

"No," I said. "Please, I just got them back. Oh, God, Mum, Dad. Mattie said you were dead, killed in a car accident."

"Yes, well. That's what the idiot over there told us, too. But it was his way of trying to get you to show. He thought you'd turn up at our funeral, and then he'd nab you there."

"Enough. Take them and the children out. I'll deal with them later."

Mum placed Maya's feet back on the floor and tugged Maya behind her body. Dad did the same with Cody.

"Mummy," Maya wailed. "I'm not leaving my mummy," Maya said, stomping her foot on the floor.

"Ha! I'm afraid so, daughter of mine."

"You're not my daddy. Talon is," she stated.

David's upper lip rose. "Get them out of here. Now!"

"I'll see you soon. It's going to be fine." How many times had I said that? I could only hope it was true. The great part was that I knew my parents would do anything to protect Maya and Cody, and they knew that I would understand that.

"Be smart and safe, sweetheart," Dad said.

Oh, God. Just like Mattie.

Snot a block—Mattie and Julian.

I nodded, tears threatening again. "Be good kids for your grandparents." I kissed Maya and Cody on their temple. "I love you both," I said, and it was then I saw for the first time tears in Cody's eyes.

"Love you, too, Mummy." Maya smiled. Cody gave me a chin lift…just like his father.

Mum hugged me close and whispered, "Don't give in."

"I never will." Not when I had Talon.

She picked up Maya. Dad placed his arm around Cody's shoulders, and they walked silently from the room with two guards, the one who came in with them, and one of Rocko's men. Thankfully, the one who'd eyed Maya stayed behind.

I slumped back onto the couch.

"No, no, Zara. Come and sit in this chair." David gestured to the chair Pervy Guy placed a foot in front of David's desk.

I rolled my eyes, hopped up, walked over, and sank into the wooden chair. Pervy Guy came to stand behind me. Hairs on the back of my neck rose. I looked over my shoulder at him and he grinned down at me.

"What's your name?" I couldn't keep calling him Pervy Guy, and I needed a name to seek my vengeance on.

"Call me Jeff."

I doubted that was his real name.

David stood, walked around the table, and stopped in front of me. My heart rate accelerated as *Jeff* grabbed both my arms and pulled then roughly behind the chair, holding them in place.

I winced. "Why all the fuss for me, David?"

He laughed. "I never like to let anything go, Zara, you knew this."

Whack. He slapped me across my already sore face.

"Obviously, I hired the wrong people to find you, for it to take this long. Wasn't it lucky these men contacted me and said they'd found my wife? You really should have turned up at the funeral, Zara. I might not have been as mad as I am now," he said, leaning over me with his hands on the armrests of the chair, our noses nearly touching. "But then again, you have really pissed me off." He leaned back.

Whack. A hit to the other side of my face forced my head around. Agony pounded in my face and heart.

At least he was being kind enough to not hit me in the same spot.

I licked my lip and tasted blood.

I don't know if I'm going to get out of this.

"Six years, Zara. You left me for six long years, and if you hadn't, I would have been fine. My plan would have been over by now, and I would be a rich man. But I'm not, all because of you."

Whack. I slumped in the chair and gasped, not just from David hitting me, but from being held in place, my shoulders and arms protesting against the angle Jeff had them in.

"Sit her up," David ordered. He sat back on the edge of his desk, eyeing me. It was starting to get a little hard to see; my face was already swelling. I felt the urge to vomit. The taste of blood and the pain churned in my stomach.

"So, we have a daughter."

I couldn't help but laugh. Now, he wanted to talk.

"Oof," I released with a gasp as David punched me in the stomach. I tried to calm my breathing, but ended up in a coughing fit. I spat blood onto the floor.

"Do not laugh at me." He opened a drawer in the desk and pulled out a wet wipe, wiping away my blood from his hands. He pulled out a knife, stalked back around, and in one move, he stabbed it into my leg.

I bit my lip, trying to stop my scream, but it still escaped.

He pulled it out slowly and ordered, "Rest her up a bit. I need to make some calls, and then we'll talk again."

I was roughly pulled from the chair just before I passed out.

CHAPTER TWENTY-THREE

TALON

"What the fuck is going on here?" Rocko yelled, and stood from his desk. I stormed into his office in the nightclub he owned around midmorning. Griz, Deanna, Violet, and three other brothers were following close behind. Blue had called, informing me that he and Warden were at the hospital with Mattie and Julian. They weren't allowed in Pick's room, under doctor's orders. But he reassured me, as soon as no one was watching, he'd be in there.

With a lift of my hand, the three brothers slipped outta the room and closed the door, keeping an eye open for trouble that could come our way.

"What do you know, arsehole?" Deanna snapped. She stood next to Vi, both holding their hands on their hips.

"Sorry, sweetheart; I don't know what you're talking about."

I pulled a gun from under my Hawks vest and pointed it at his head.

He stood with his hands up in front of him. I followed his movements.

"Where are my boys?" he asked.

Violet scoffed. "You need new brothers, Rocko. They're all a bunch of pussies and incapacitated."

"Talon, what's the meaning of this? You want war? Is that it?"

"Two of your men have taken my woman and kids to hand her over to her ex, who beat and raped her. You tell me, do you want fuckin' war?"

"I know nothing about this. They have obviously gone out on their own. Who are they?"

"The guys that were with you last night," Deanna said.

Rocko smiled.

"What the fuck are you smiling at?" I roared.

Waving his hands he said, "Sorry, shit. I know it ain't a smiling matter. But your woman…" He smiled again.

"What?" Griz growled.

"She warned me last night that I needed to find new friends. Goddamn, she was right, and after just one glance, she picked it. Fuck. I should've never let them in. I was taking a risk on them. Other brothers had warned me, but I didn't listen. We needed new recruits. The Monty's motorcycle club from Melbourne wants our territory. Crap, I was only with them last night to see how they ran, and I didn't like what I saw. I was gonna cut them."

"How'd they learn about my woman and her ex?"

"I was the one who told Rocko. Fuck," Griz swore. "I'd asked him to keep his ear to the ground, see if he heard anything new. Shit, I didn't think."

"Jesus Christ!" I yelled. "Jesus Christ." I turned and put a hole in the wall the size of my fist.

"I'm sorry, brother," Griz said.

"Fuck, man, but it ain't your fault. You weren't to know," I answered, leaning one hand up against the wall.

I couldn't lose her. Cody and Maya...

It would kill me to lose any of them, most of all the three of them together.

I'd wasted so much time stuffin' around and waiting, trying not to scare her off. But I knew she'd been watchin' me the whole time as well. I saw the looks she gave me, the secret smiles that drove me fuckin' nuts. The way she'd blush at my words, the way her breathing would become faster when I was around.

I should have moved in sooner.

I should have claimed her months ago.

I'd thought the dicks in the brotherhood were crazy

when they'd let their old ladies run their lives. Blinded by stupid love. I swore I'd never let myself fall again…never.

Until Zara. Until I fuckin' walked down that hallway to see a hot piece of arse standing there, glaring at me in a pink kitten nightie and combat fuckin' boots.

I was a goner.

From that day on, I knew I'd let Zara do anything.

She could talk, bitch, and complain about shit and it wouldn't faze me. She could harp about me swearin' around the kids, and still it wouldn't bother me.

Nothin' would, as long as she was at my side to do all that.

I had to find her. Them.

Jesus. The kids. I'd already missed out on enough of Cody's life. I wasn't missin' out on any more. And sweet Maya. There was so much more I wanted to learn about them both, so much I wanted to teach them.

I needed them all back.

They are my family.

And I fuckin' love them.

"Do you know where they have taken my family?" I asked Rocko.

"No. But I'll look into it. Maybe one of the brothers knows something." Rocko sat back down at the desk.

"You know I'll kill them."

"So be it. They are no longer Vicious."

My mobile rang and I answered, "What?"

"Nothing. I've got nothing," Blue said.

"Is Pick talkin'?"

"Yeah, he's talking, telling me lots of shit. None of it is any use to find them, brother. Cops have been. They want a statement on what went on in the house."

"Fuck. Has Mattie or anyone said anything?"

"Nothing, I told them to wait to hear from you. But you know the cops, brother. They won't wait long."

"Tell them to say it was self-defence. I had Mattie and Julian stayin' at my house. Pick called in and he found Vic holding them, ready to kill them. Vic was a hater of gays. Didn't like the way I was running things. No one says shit about my woman and the kids. We deal with this in-house. I'll be doing the clean-up."

"But the cops could help."

"No. They'll only hold me back."

"Right. On it. Then what?"

"Tell Matthew and Julian to head back to the compound—"

"Already have. They won't leave." Blue laughed. "They don't trust me and Warden around Pick. He saved them, brother. They're saving him back."

"Christ. All right, leave them there, and Warden, you get to the compound and see what they've found. Talk to Travis and see what's he's got. I'm heading to Vi's work."

"Right. Done," he said, then hung up.

I turned to Rocko. "Keep me in the know," I said with

a chin lift. *In other words, if you don't, I'll fuck you over.* He nodded his understanding.

"I hope you find 'em, Talon. She's a rare beauty."

"I know. I fuckin' know. So are the kids. Let's move."

"Wait," Violet called, before I opened the door.

"What?" Rocko asked her; she was staring down at him.

"Do you know what they drive? Licence plate numbers, where they live? Maybe they're stupid enough to either use their own cars or take them to their place?"

"Great thinkin', sugar." He got up from his chair and went to a file cabinet to the right of his desk. "I had to shift my paperwork here while the office at our compound was getting detailed. Fuckin' lucky I did," he explained as he searched through the drawers.

Hell. How long did it take to find the information?

I just hoped these fuckers were just that dumb. And thank fuck my sister was here using her brain.

"Here." He thrust the files toward Deanna, the closest to him. "All the info I have on Jefferson and Zane. And while you're searching through it, I'll still keep looking here."

"'Preciate it."

Once outside, I sent my other brothers out searchin' the streets while Griz, Hell Mouth, Vi, and I got back into my Camaro to drive to Vi's station.

With the information we had, I felt a little lighter. The fist around my heart wasn't squeezing as tightly.

I just hoped it was going to lead us somewhere where my family was.

Payback was needing to happen, and I was looking forward to it.

There was no way I was gonna be some pansy-arse and pray…even if I wanted to.

Shit.

Fuck.

Why the hell not? Anything was worth it for them.

Yeah, um, God...

WE STORMED into Violet's work. Funnily enough, it was the first time I'd ever set foot in there. Things had to change. A lot of things. Violet booted up her computers while Deanna and Griz were talkin' quietly in a hushed tone, but I knew what it would be about. He was trying to reassure her, and I knew she wouldn't want that from him. Deanna was one hard chick to crack. Griz would have his work cut out for him when he got his act together. I should hurry him the fuck up—'cause you never knew what could happen.

"Anything?" I asked.

"Talon, I'm not that frigging fast, give me a minute." Violet groaned.

I paced in front of one of her desks while she worked on the computer; her fingers flew across the keyboard. I wondered where Zara sat while she worked. She hadn't been there long, but I knew she'd already brought some of herself into the business. The yellow sunflowers that sat on the windowsill. The scenic picture of the woods with a ray of sunshine shining through that hung on the wall. The colourful rug that sat in the middle of the floor. She'd always brightened up a place.

"I'll send Chuck to their houses, but I doubt they're there. They would have taken them to David straight away so they could be paid." She picked up the phone and rang her employee.

Griz walked over to me. "She's freaking. I'm worried she'll lose it soon."

I nodded. "She's not the only one." I sighed and ran a hand through my hair. "The thing I've noticed, though, is that Hell Mouth relies on Zara in more ways than one. Deanna not only helped Zara outta her past, but I'm sure it was the other way around as well. Not sure kitten knows that though unless she does and carries that burden, as well as Deanna." I looked over my shoulder to Deanna as she perched her arse on the end of Vi's desk. She looked in pain. "Anyone can fuckin' see that woman has been through some shit from that big iced wall she has built around her, and right now, it seems only Zara has a key."

I turned to Griz. "Good luck, brother; you're gonna need it." My phone rang and I grabbed it outta the pocket of my jeans, answering with, "Speak."

"Just got back to the compound. The brothers have nothing. No one's called in with shit, Talon. How's your end?"

"Violet, how we doing?" I was feeling antsy. I needed to be doing something instead of talking shit with Griz, or standing around doing crap. I felt useless, and it fuckin' hurt when it was my family out there in trouble.

"Zip. I've got Chuck on the line. There's no one at their houses. Their cars are in their frigging drives. I've got nothing else to go on. I'm sorry."

"Jesus Christ," I whispered.

"I'm guessing it's not good," Blue said on the other end of the phone.

"No. Fuck, brother. We have to find them—"

"Talon, wait," Blue snapped.

"Blue?" I heard talking in the background, but I didn't know what was being fuckin' said. "Brother?"

"Shit. Shit, boss, we've got them. Travis just came in. He's fucking found where they are."

"Text me the address. I'll meet you there," I said, and turned to the others. "Travis got a location. Let's go."

"Thank God." Deanna sighed.

"Christ, yes," Griz growled.

"Talon, wait," Violet called.

"What, woman? I gotta get my family."

"You and Griz need my guns. If the bullets are traced, I'm covered for being a PI. You're not."

I closed my eyes.

My sister was protecting me.

"I want one too," Deanna said.

"No way, darlin'. You get a taser," Griz barked and handed her a black taser from his back pocket.

"Seriously?" she said with an eye roll.

I ignored them as Violet approached holding three guns. She handed one to Griz and then one to me. I looked her in the eye and said, "There could be a lotta people goin' down today, Vi. You ready for this?"

"Fuck yeah." She smiled.

"Let's move then." I smiled back.

CHAPTER TWENTY-FOUR

ZARA

I woke lying on a double four-poster bed in a dark room. I could see the sun shining through the gaps in the blinds. That told me it was still daytime, but I didn't have a clue what hour it was, or how long I'd been asleep.

I was sore all over. I needed water and something to eat, but I doubted I'd be able to keep it down.

Where was my family?

What was going to happen next?

I sat up slowly, wincing when pain stabbed through my head and leg. I looked down at the wound and found that someone had changed me into slip-on pyjama pants.

Why?

The door opened, and in walked a young girl around the age of sixteen with long red curly hair and a freckled face. She was short but slim, too skinny, actually. She carried a tray with a glass and a bowl upon it.

"Oh, you're awake." She smiled, but it didn't reach her eyes; it was all fake, a show. "Good. You'll be wanting some food and water, yes?"

I nodded. What was such a young girl doing in the house with David? She set the tray on the bed beside me. I took the glass with shaking hands and sipped it. The water helped my parched throat.

I looked to the door that she'd left open.

"You won't make it," she whispered as she stood beside the bed. A look of dread passed over her features.

What? Was she a mind reader?

"W-who are you?" I asked.

"I was homeless until David took me in." She glanced at the door, and then back to me. Bending over, so we were inches apart, she whispered, "You need to get out of here. He's going to kill you."

My eyes widened. Why was she warning me? I controlled my eye roll. *God, doesn't she think I already know that?*

"How can I get out?" I asked.

She shrugged. "That, I don't know."

"I wouldn't without my family anyway."

Her head cocked to the side. "Smart or stupid you are, but I can't work out which one. I know I'm stupid because I keep staying here. So maybe you're the same?" She smiled sadly.

Probably.

"Josie, what are you doing in here?" David came through the door.

Josie nearly jumped out of her skin, her cheeks turning a deep shade of red. "Nothing, Daddy. Um, I mean, I brought our guest some supper."

Oh, my flipping God. Was this for real? I mean I'd always wanted to role-play where Talon was a pirate and I was a damsel in distress…kind of like now.

But their roles were just fruited up.

Jesus, why hadn't I seen how crazy this fucktard was from the start?

He stalked across the room. Josie backed up until she hit the wall. "I told you not to call me daddy around people," he hissed through clenched teeth, and then slapped her across the face.

She whimpered and sunk to the floor. "I'm sorry, David."

"Don't be an arse," I said. He turned to face me.

Better me than an innocent girl.

He grabbed me by my hair and dragged me from the bed. I cried out when I landed on my knees in front of him.

"Don't," Josie screamed. She jumped onto his back, clawing at his face. He swore and flipped her off. She landed beside me with a *thunk*. He kicked her in her side and she groaned.

I punched him in the balls. It was his turn to groan, bending at the waist.

"Run," I yelled to Josie, but she didn't move, staying curled up in her protective ball.

"Jefferson," David called. In ran Jeff. "Take my *wife* to my office. I'll deal with her in a minute."

"You are nothing but a perverted cocksucker, David. Or should I call you daddy too? Isn't that what you like, you hairy sac sucker?" I yelled.

"Take her, now," David barked. Jeff dragged me up and threw me over his shoulder. I clenched my teeth at the pain.

We moved down a hallway, but I noticed David walk out of the room behind us and lock the door. I smiled to myself. I'd pissed him off that much? I guess he wanted to deal with me first. At least that left Josie alone... for now.

In the office, Jeff threw me onto the couch.

"Leave," David ordered.

Jeff smirked down at me, gave me a tap on the head, and left, closing the door behind him. David turned the lock into place.

He started pacing the room. "I used to think when I

got you back we could have worked this out. But you've changed."

"Lucky for me, eh?" I sat up straighter and wondered why I wasn't bleeding through the pants I had on. I felt my leg where David had stabbed me. It was covered by some sort of tape.

"Shut the hell up," he screamed. I felt like telling him he screamed like a girl, but I didn't think that would go down well. Though, my chances were getting slimmer by the second.

I love you, Talon. Tears threatened.

All I could do now was pray that he got here in time to save the children and my parents.

"I should have never been with you, David." I laughed. "I thought I knew what love was, but I didn't. Because now I know what love is. The love I feel for Talon is bigger than anything I've felt before—"

He ran at me, grabbing my shoulders, and roughly shook me. "Shut up. Shut up. Shut up. You are nothing." He spun away and walked to the desk.

Oh, shit.

He yanked open a drawer and pulled out a gun. "I would never have wasted my time in finding you, but your life insurance is going to make it worth it."

Say what, now?

"Um, hold on a second." I giggled. "Have you thought

this through? Won't the insurance people know something's up if I'm riddled with bullets?"

Why am I helping him? Jeesh.

It was then I realised that I wasn't scared of David. I was no longer scared. What was in front of me was an old, mean man and nothing else.

"The police wouldn't question a break-in, where my dear wife was killed defending our home. Well, not home—seems you made me fucking travel a state away to kill you," he yelled and then shook his head. "Instead they broke into our new holiday warehouse here in Melbourne. Isn't it wonderful? I get a dead wife. I get money and a new place. Yes, I think I'll live here… with my two daughters."

"No!" I screamed.

He raised the gun and fired.

My body bounced back into the couch. I looked down as pain throbbed through my arm; blood started to soak my tee.

Damn it, I liked this one.

"Practice shot," he smirked. He raised the gun again.

CHAPTER TWENTY-FIVE

TALON

I'd organised to stop a block away, in an old, unused supermarket car park. I didn't want to rouse suspicion with Harley pipes, as well as all the large fuckin' cars pulling up to the warehouse.

I got out of my car just as twenty or so Harleys were roaring down the street and pulling in to stop. Blue was the first over to me, Griz, Deanna, and Violet.

"What's the plan?" he asked.

"We need to be fast, get in and get out. The warehouse is a block away at the end of a dead-end street. Not much goes on in these parts, so there shouldn't be any witnesses we'd need to buy off."

Fuck. I felt like I was wasting time standing there explaining. All I wanted to do was get in there, kill the fucker, and get my family back.

Violet stepped forward and rested her hand on my arm. "We go in on foot from here. We don't want them knowing we're coming." She looked over Blue's shoulder to a white sedan pulling into the car park. It stopped just behind the Harleys. "Good, just in time." She grinned as Warden got out of the car, went to the back of it, and opened the trunk. "Everyone needs to swap over their weapons for one of ours," Violet shouted to my brothers.

"Shit, Vi." I closed my eyes. "How the fuck are you going to explain firing off twenty or so guns to the cops?"

She shrugged. "We'll deal with that when the time comes." I shook my head as she added, "Do you think Zara would want her man in jail after just saving her? No. Do it for her, Talon."

"Do I get a fuckin' gun now?" Deanna asked.

"No," Griz growled. "You stick with me, princess."

She sighed loudly and rolled her eyes. "Fine. But I want a piece of him."

"We'll see," I said. I wanted him first. My hands itched to choke the fucker for layin' his hands on my family in the first place. "Right, let's load up and move out," I called.

VIOLET HAD me send Warden in first to remove—if there were any—cameras. Not that I believed a large motherfucker like Warden would get in there undetected, but he came back saying the coast was clear.

I spread my brothers out so we had the whole warehouse covered. I went straight to the front door with Griz, Deanna, and Violet. Then Blue came running around from the side to inform me, "We've taken out five men."

Then why the fuck wasn't the front covered?

I gave a chin lift in response and tried the front door. It was locked. I took a step back, ready to kick it in when Deanna stepped forward and knocked. I sent her a 'what the fuck' look.

Seconds later, the front door was opened, and one of Rocko's men, still in a betraying Vicious vest, stood there.

"Fuck," he hissed. He went to grab a two-way at his waist, but Deanna punched him in the face. He teetered back. Blue jumped him and held him to the ground.

"I'm sure Rocko wants to deal with this fucker himself." Blue grinned. "You guys go. I'll find something to tie him up with," he said while emptying the dick of weapons.

I bolted for the stairs, just as my other men came through the back door and went searchin' through the bottom area.

Taking three steps at a time, I climbed the stairs with the others following.

A gunshot sounded in the distance.

"Shit, shit," Deanna chanted.

We reached a hallway. I signalled for everyone to stay quiet and keep their eyes open. I opened the first door… nothing. Griz got to the second just as another of Rocko's men was walking out. He reached for his gun as Griz knocked him out with one punch.

"Leave him. One of the brothers will deal," I whispered.

Vi was at the next door to the right; she opened it, but nothing again. I wasn't there on a fuckin' scenic tour, so I took no notice of what was in the room and moved on.

The fourth door was locked. Violet pulled something out from her back jeans pocket and started working the lock; within seconds, it clicked open. She moved out of the way. I held the door handle and turned it. I threw it open while I stepped in with my gun raised.

A gasp, a sob, and a frightened squeal were what I heard first.

I looked around the darkened room and saw four bodies huddled in the right-hand corner.

"Dad?"

My eyes closed upon hearing Cody's voice. I lowered my gun, knowing Vi and Deanna had my back. I wasn't sure where Griz was.

"Told ya he'd come," Cody said with pride.

"Talon," Maya cried as she ran at me. I had enough time to brace as her little body hit me. I picked her up and hugged her close, gesturing to Cody to come to me.

"Richard? Nancy?" Deanna asked.

"Why, hey there, Deanna girl," a man said as he stepped forward into the hallway light.

"Oh, my God." Deanna gasped, tears in her eyes. I studied the man; he was an older image of Matthew.

"My, my, it's so good to see you, Deanna, and in the flesh, instead of on Skype." A woman stepped around Richard…fuck, she was an older image of my woman. "And you're just a hot piece of eye candy." She smiled, looking up at me.

Violet and Deanna chuckled. Griz came running into the room, and in his arms was a young teenage girl.

"Found her in a room. She's unconscious but alive." He laid her on the bed.

"Have you seen Zara?" I asked.

"Oh, my. No wonder my girl couldn't resist you with a voice like that."

Richard sighed. "Nance, focus. We saw her earlier, but that was a few hours ago. We don't know where she is."

Another gunshot sounded not far from where we were.

"Fuck," I hissed. I put Maya on her feet. "Stay here

with your grandparents. Deanna, you gotta stay here with the girl in case she's gonna be trouble."

"Sure, boss," she said, taking out her taser. She looked itchin' to try that out.

"Keep 'em safe," I said to Richard as I handed him my back-up gun.

"Oh, sure, he gets a gun," Deanna complained.

Richard nodded when Nancy piped up about something regardin' me and grammar. I ignored it and knelt down to the kids. "It's gonna be good. I'll find your momma, baby girl, and then we can get outta here."

"I know you will." Maya smiled and patted me on the face.

"Good luck, Dad, and kill that fucker," Cody said.

"Boy, language," I growled, gave them both a peck on their heads, and ran from the room.

Another gunshot, but at least that time, I was able to pinpoint the location. It was the last fuckin' door at the end of the hall.

I tried the handle. Locked. I didn't waste time for Violet to pick it; instead, I kicked it open. With the gun held up, and with Vi and Griz at my back, I stepped in.

Fuckin' motherfucker.

I saw my woman on a couch, bleeding.

Shit, there was fuckin' blood everywhere.

"Who the hell are you?" David asked.

As I stared him down, he backed up, and Violet ran to Zara.

"Tell me she's breathing," I said.

"H-honey?" my woman said, but then started coughing.

"Christ, Talon. We have to get her outta here. She's got three gunshot wounds, and she's been beaten."

"You are not taking her," David yelled.

"Back the fuck up," I roared. I stalked toward him. "You bloodied my woman, you beat her, raped her, and fuckin' shot her. Fuck!"

Fury. All I could feel was fury. This fucker did not deserve it quick and painless.

He was going to pay.

He went to pick up the gun he'd dropped on the desk when we'd bound into the room, but I got there first and shot his hand away.

"Damn it!" he screamed, holding his hand to his chest.

"Talon! We have to go, and now," Violet screamed.

"Griz, take him. Clean this. I'm gettin' my woman outta here."

Griz smiled. "Sure, brother."

I stalked over to the couch. "Jesus, babe," I whispered.

"I-I k-knew you'd come. Kids? Parents?"

"They're safe. Now let's get you safe." There was no time for an ambo, so as gently as I could, I picked her up in my arms, but still, she cried out.

Pain laced through my heart.

"Vi, clear the way. Make sure the kids don't see."

"On it," she said, running from the room.

"H-honey..."

"Yeah, kitten?"

"I-I don't know...if this is gonna work. I-if I can—"

"Shit, kitten. Don't. You're gonna be all right, you're gonna be good. Fuck, babe. I know you're gonna be good 'cause I love you, and my fuckin' love for you is strong enough to keep you that way. So let's get you fixed, yeah?"

"Y-yeah, honey. You k-know, I love your alpha arse too." She smiled up at me and then passed out.

AS SOON AS we reached the hospital, they took her away. They took her from my arms and told me to stay. The cops were called; still, my brothers got there first. The waiting room looked like a party at the compound. But instead of havin' a good ol' drunken time, everyone was sober and sombre.

I sat in a chair with my head in my hands as they worked over my woman. Zara's parents had the kids at her house, with more of my brothers watchin' them. They were waiting to hear from me. I just hoped to fuck I had good news to tell them.

No. It will be great, fan-fuckin'-tastic news that I'll tell them!

Griz was deflecting the cops, tellin' them what had gone down at the warehouse... well, our story of it. He told them that Zara had been kidnapped by her crazy ex and that when we turned up, David had taken off. We hadn't bothered chasin', 'cause we had to get her to the hospital. It was lucky enough that we had a witness, the young girl Josie, whom David had held hostage for the last three years. When Billy had brought her in, she'd said that she was willin' to tell the cops whatever we wanted, and she did. That, at least, brought me more time to sit and wait for my woman to get fixed. Though the cops said they'd still need my statement at a later date, as well as—how'd they put it? 'Miss Edgingway's, if she pulls through.'

If.

If she fuckin' pulled through.

That was when I punched a cop, swingin', and yellin' to get the fuck out. Blue had to pull me off him. The cop told Violet later that he wouldn't be pressing charges because he understood.

Not that I gave a fuck.

By the time the doctors came out, I had a child in each arm, and Zara's parents were sitting with me. They decided not to wait at Zara's house after all and came in after showering and changing. I couldn't blame them.

Deanna had turned up earlier, screamin' that she missed out on her shot, that she missed out on her retaliation on the fucker. That was when I'd whispered, "Not yet, you ain't."

She fuckin' grinned with pure glee and then sat her arse down to wait it out with us.

The doctor teetered backwards when she spotted the waiting room full of bikers.

"Uh...family of Zara Edgingway?"

"That's us," I said, standing. Zara's parents held the tired children close.

"Oh, okay. I just wanted to say she's through the surgery, and it looks like she's going to be okay."

I sank to my knees, and for the second time that day, I fuckin' prayed my thanks for savin' my life. 'Cause I knew I wouldn't have a life without my kitten in it.

EPILOGUE

FOUR MONTHS LATER

ZARA

I'd been out of the hospital for two months when my mum turned up at Talon's house… though I should say our house because my man, being his bossy alpha self, had moved me in while I was still in the hospital.

My man loved to control.

But still, he had my heart in hand. He knew I'd be more than happy to have my family close, and I was.

Not only had my mum showed, but my father and

Josie, who was my now adopted sister. She was still one mixed-up girl, but who could blame her after living with David for three years, and what he'd put her through?

I told her I'd help her along the way to recovery because we were sisters now. That was the first time I'd seen her smile. Not only had she attached herself to my parents and me, but she'd formed a bond with Maya, Cody, and Billy, the cookie-loving biker, one of Talon's brothers, who'd been her saviour by taking her to the hospital.

Mattie and Julian (who also joined the community of Ballarat and moved into my old place across the road from the compound) arrived with Deanna, Griz, and Blue.

Mum strode on through the door first with a small kiss to my cheek and hands full of dishes. Heck, it wasn't only her hands full but it was obvious she'd roped everyone else into brining something as well.

"What's this about?" I asked the last person through the door, my brother.

He rolled his eyes and said, "Just go with it, she's been cooking all day muttering about how her baby girl isn't eating enough. Apparently, you need more protein and vitamins to help you heal so you can give her grandbabies."

With wide eyes, I asked, "Please don't tell me she said that to everyone who walked in the front door just now?"

"Okay, I won't." He laughed, kissed my cheek and followed the rest to the kitchen.

It was then Talon walked from down the hall into the living room, where I was still standing with the front door open.

"Kitten, you're lettin' out all the warmth. What you doin', woman?"

"They just turned up. I didn't know they were coming and my mum's told everyone I need to heal to give her grandbabies… why are you smiling? You do know she'll be on your case soon because you're the one who has to impregnate me. Oh my God, she'll want to know things like when I'm ovulating, or I've got my period so she can work it out… she used to be a nurse; she's going to make our lives hell if she's already thinking about grandbabies." I'd been ecstatic when my parents told me they were moving to Ballarat… now I wasn't so sure.

"Babe." My man rolled his eyes at me. I snorted and shook my head at him. He didn't know; he hadn't been around her long enough to know my mum was… viciously crazy. Talon walked over to me, he took the front door out of my hand and closed it. Then he leaned in and kissed me soundly. So soundly I forgot what I was freaking out over.

"Wow," I uttered.

"Damn right. Now get in the kitchen and help get the

food ready so we can eat, they can leave, we can put the kids to bed and then we can fuck like rabbits."

Biting my bottom lip, I admitted, "That sounds like a good plan."

He chuckled, touched his lips to mine and shooed me into the kitchen. I looked over my shoulder and asked, "How come you can't get in here and help as well?"

"Kitten." He chuckled and then said, "I have a dick, and all men with dicks sit back, drink, and watch their women do the work."

"Cheers to that," my dad yelled.

"Richard, don't you even think about doing nothing. Get your butt over here and carve this meat up. Talon can have a break, that good-looking man has been helping our baby girl nonstop."

"Jesus, Nance. I should get a break for just putting up with you."

Stopping in the doorway of the kitchen, I turned back to Talon and bulged my eyes out. As if he didn't care my family was crazy, he just smiled back with a shrug.

Maybe he was crazier for putting up with it all.

Or he loved me as much as I loved him.

Smiling to myself, I stalked in to help Mum before things got out of hand.

An hour later we all surrounded the twelve-seater kitchen table. Griz, Deanna, Blue, Mattie, and Julian all sat on one side, my parents, the quiet Josie and the children on the other. Talon and I were at opposite ends. The food had been consumed and I loved it all. Mum always made a fantastic roast. Even the guys were raving about how good it was.

Watching everyone interact was amazing. Having my parents there and alive even better; seeing the way they had already bonded with their grandchildren, Maya and Cody, was something special. It brought tears to my eyes. The day would forever be in my memories.

Talon suddenly stood from the table. He cleared his throat. "The real reason I asked everyone here—"

"Wait, you organised this?" I interrupted, confused.

He smiled widely. "Of course, kitten." He started walking toward me, behind my parents and children.

Had I done something wrong?

Was he getting rid of me in front of everyone?

Was my heart about to explode in my chest?

If it did, it was all his fault.

Talon stopped at my side. He leaned over, took my shaking hand in his, and then… Oh my God, he got to one knee. My free hand went over my mouth, tears filled my eyes, and my body started to tremble with nerves.

"Kitten, no more stuffing around. The day I thought I'd lost you was… fuckin' painful. I know from then, hell not even that, from the day you moved onto the street, I knew I'd want to claim you in every way. You, Kitten, are my life, you're my soul, and I'd be nothing without you. Would you do me the honour of becomin' my wife?"

Speechless. I couldn't say anything, I couldn't move. I was in shock. This fine specimen of a badarse man wanted me in his future. He wanted me to be his wife.

Holy crap.

Talon Marcus wanted us to be his future.

Just like I had, but I'd never, not ever thought he would ask me to marry him.

"Kitten, you're killin' me here."

"Iloveyousomuch," I mumbled behind my hand.

"For the love of God, talk normal and give the poor man an answer," my dad yelled.

"YES!" I screamed and then jumped him.

He landed with a thud on the floor with me on top of him. My mouth attacked his, and he took it all with a chuckle.

Everyone started clapping and cheering.

I pulled back so I could see Talon's warm, soft, happy eyes.

Maya was the first on the Talon and Zara huddle; she climbed onto my back, leaned over my shoulder, and said, "Now you really will be my daddy."

TWO MONTHS LATER

"Talon," I moaned.

"Jesus, kitten." He groaned as I rolled my hips. We were in his room, at his...*our* house. The kids were at my parents', and it was time for us to have a private party for two. He was sitting up against the headboard, naked as the day he was born. I was just as naked, besides some rocking heels my man had bought me for my birthday last week.

I was working my inner-cowgirl magic, riding him like I was meant to.

Leaning forward, I kissed him.

I was never going to get enough of him.

Never.

"Babe," he groaned.

"Not yet, honey."

"Fuck, kitten."

"Not yet," I uttered through clenched teeth. "Oh, God, honey. Now." I gripped the headboard behind him as he pounded his cum into me, and I climaxed around him.

Exhausted, I rested my head against his shoulder, breathing hard.

"Christ, woman. We are never doin' that position again. I come too fuckin' quick."

I giggled. "Hell to the no. I love taking control."

"Only in the bedroom you can, and only when I let you," he growled.

"Whatever," I said, pulling back so he could see my eyes roll. He grinned. I got out of bed and went into the en suite to clean up. When I came back out, Talon was lying down with a sheet covering his bottom half. I ran and leapt right onto the bed. He chuckled at my antics. I turned off the lamp on the bedside table and snuggled in. Then I wiggled as close as I could to him, knowing he'd curl me into his arms just like he always did.

"You happy, kitten?"

"More than happy…but worried."

He laughed. "No need to be, 'ca I'll be here right alongside you. Always."

"I know, honey. That's why I love you."

"And I you, babe. Now sleep."

"Yes, boss." And I squealed when he slapped my behind.

I was worried because that morning at my doctor's appointment, we found out we were having twins. Talon had grinned down at my shocked face and said, "Fuck yeah. Kitten, when I do something, I do it good, and you got it good."

That was still debatable.

I had been just getting over the fact that we weren't sure I'd be able to have children after David had shot me twice in the stomach. You could say that Talon was over the frigging moon we'd be having a child together. He'd said that I'd been through enough shit in my life to last me till I was old and grey, and now that we were finally over the speed hump, we could live our lives to the fullest, each and every day.

Well, our lives would certainly be filled.

Of course, after the news, I ran and cried on Deanna's shoulder, telling her that Talon had supersonic sperm and that he'd sonic-ed his way into my… fandola, and shot me up with twins.

Her response was, "Well, fuck me."

I thought another hot-crisis issue would have gotten her out of her funk. But it hadn't.

She was worrying me because these days I hardly saw her, and when I did, she always seemed to have something on her mind… only she wasn't sharing.

It was if she'd been altered when I'd been taken, and it wasn't something she was getting over. Though, I still doubted it was that alone. Something else was in her head, and I was going to get to the bottom of it.

We'd been keeping a close eye on Maya and Cody since the incident, but they seemed to be handling it okay. We'd had Cody every second weekend until that stopped and we got full custody.

And that was because Cody had rung in the middle of the night recently, and we'd found just what his mum and stepfather had been up to.

Talon woke and picked up his phone. I'd woken when I heard a gruff, "Talk." And then he paused and said in a growled voice, "They're what?" I sat up quickly beside Talon and placed my hand on his back. "I'll be there soon."

He climbed out of bed and donned a tee and jeans before he turned to me and hissed, "Bianca and fuckhead are havin' a party. That was Cody. Let me just say it's not a party a kid his age should be witness to. We're gonna go get 'im." I was out of bed in seconds and threw on jeans and a hooded, long-sleeved top.

Maya was already having a sleepover at my parents' house, so there was nothing to delay us getting into Talon's car and driving the ten minutes to Bianca's house.

As we drove down the long driveway, we could already hear the music pounding from the house. I knew nothing of Bianca's new husband other than the fact he was someone who had money, and Talon called him a dick.

Talon skidded to stop. He handed me a small devise and said, "It's a Go-Pro. I need you to film what we see in there and we'll be takin' that fucker to court. I want full custody of my son."

"Okay, honey." I nodded. He kissed me hard and quickly and got out of the car. I was out and at his side as we stalked up to the front door.

Talon turned to me, his face dark and scary. "You'll be

safe, they'd know not to touch you, or I'd fuck with them. Stay close though. We get in, get Cody and get out."

"I'm with you." I smiled.

"Fuck, how'd I get so lucky?" His lips pressed to my forehead before he spun, grabbed the front door handle and slammed it open.

Hmm, I guess it isn't locked.

"What. The. Fuck," Talon roared when he stepped in. I came around him with the Go-Pro held high and I soon found myself wishing I couldn't see.

In the large open-plan living room in front of us were…bodies. So many bodies and they were all naked, rolling around each other and doing things that shouldn't be happening when a child was in the house.

Suddenly the music was cut off, and Bianca was in front of us. Thank God she had a robe on.

"What are you doing here with *her*?" she demanded.

Talon took a step forward, leaned in and snarled in his ex's face, "Get rid of your 'tude, Bianca and tell me, do you think this situation is good for our son to be near?"

She rolled her eyes. "He's up in his room, I told him to stay there. He won't see anything."

"What's going on, darling?" A man of about fifty walked up.

Oh God. He was as naked as the day he was born and it was not a pretty sight. His bulging belly and chest hair were enough to put me off my food for a year, but when his hand ran along his small prick while eyeing me I just about dry heaved.

Talon was in front of me to hide the sight. Thank Jesus. I arched my hand around him with the Go-Pro so I could still capture everything.

"You look at my woman with your hand on your tiny dick again, I will fuckin' end you." My man was tense, he wanted to fight and take lives, but I knew he would hold himself back because his son was in the house. A house he should never have been in.

"Honey, I like the way you think, but that's not good for the camera."

He looked over his shoulder and smirked. "We'll edit it out."

"Camera?" Bianca gasped.

Talon turned back to her and said, "Yeah, bitch. My woman just took all this shit in and now I'm takin' my son outta here without any fuckin' trouble." He crossed his arms over his chest. "You won't fight me this time, Bianca. I'm getting' full custody of Cody. You no longer exist for him. If you balk at anything, the cops will see just what goes down in here."

"He's my son, Talon."

"Not anymore," Talon growled. "No mother would do this shit with a child in the house. You just lost him, Bianca."

The stupid woman shrugged. "Go and get him. See if I care."

I stepped up. "How could you—"

"Kitten, she ain't worth it." He was right, she wasn't. Talon took my hand and we starting walking through the house.

Thankfully, we got Cody out of there without him seeing anything. When we were in the car, on our way back home, a quiet Cody asked, "Am I going back there?"

"No, Cody. Never. You're with us from now on."

His smile was bright. So bright it caused me to get teary. "Good," he said.

Turning in my seat, I told Cody, "You'll be happy with us."

His nod was immediate. "I know, Zee."

Things were now going to be full in our house, and I was looking forward to it. Of course, it wasn't always going to be roses and chocolates; we were two totally different people, arguments were bound to happen. Our first one wasn't long after I was released from the hospital, and it was regarding Pick. Mattie and Julian had told me what Pick had done for them. Talon wanted Pick gone from the brotherhood. Mattie, Julian, and I told him to give him another chance. Eventually, we'd worn him down, and he said he'd consider it. Meaning Pick was still in the brotherhood, and in the end, it was Talon and

Mattie who helped Pick cut the ties his mother had on him.

I used to wake every night while I was in the hospital, but that stopped as soon as I had Talon sleeping next to me.

I'd always have scars, but they were something that made me stronger. To prove that I was over what had happened and that I was stronger for it, I did something that scared me. I got my first tattoo to cover the smallest scar—which hurt like a mother-fruiter. And that was when Talon and I had our second argument. He didn't want my body inked. That was when I yelled, "What's good for the goose is good for the gander." His reply was, "What the fuck does that mean?" I flashed him my tattoo on my lower stomach, a picture of a hawk, and underneath it was written 'You flew into my life, but I've got my claws into yours.'

The next day, he'd come back with his own tattoo, a picture of a kitten digging its claws into his skin.

"Jesus, kitten. I can hear your brain churning again. Get to sleep. Everythin' will be good."

I smiled into the dark room and knew that everything would be good because I had my badarse biker beside me.

SNEAK PEEK — CLIMBING OUT

HAWKS MC: BALLARAT CHARTER: BOOK 2

Prologue

DEANNA

As I watched Zara and her new husband twirl on the dance floor at their wedding reception, I wanted to throw up.

Then again, I was also so fucking happy for her; maybe that was why I felt sick to my stomach.

She looked absolutely beautiful in her designer gown, even if her tiny two-month baby bump showed. It was as though she pulled her dress from a page in a princess storybook and slapped it on herself.

Bitch.

Only she deserved this happy day, and so many more

after the hell she'd been through. Even though eight months had passed, it still felt like yesterday when I'd come out of Griz's room at the compound to find Zara had been taken. The thought that I'd possibly lose my best friend shattered many things inside of me.

Yes, she pulled out of it, but I knew what something like that could cost you mentally. Sure, she seemed fine on the outside, but the inside would be a different matter.

At least she had her boss-man to take care of her, and I knew he would.

Sighing, I sat back in my chair, and even though my insides were playing turmoil, I felt myself smile. Zara would soon be whipped away for her honeymoon in Fiji, the vacation they never got to have because everything turned into crazy-arse wedding planning mode. She was so excited about it, and when she got excited, other people also joined in on her thrill ride.

From the look in boss man's eyes, I knew she'd be on her back in a matter of time. I chuckled to myself. There was no way I'd ever want to be in that situation.

Okay, so yeah, I could do with the part of being on my back, just without the being married and knocked up bit.

My eyes searched out Griz. He stood on the other side of the dance floor, casually leaning against the bar; his eyes were on me. I squeezed my legs together. Goddamn did I want that man, but he kept fighting it, and right then I was glad he did.

My life for the next seven months or so was going to be busy. I didn't need the distraction, and I knew as soon as I had my hands on Griz, I wouldn't ever want to let go.

I looked to my bag and saw the letter sticking out. I pushed it back in and zipped it up. That was the second letter; I got the first one when Zara's shit had started.

Both were like a knife to my stomach.

I thought I'd gotten rid of him from my life—obviously, that wasn't the case.

I had eight months before he came looking for me.

I could only hope my plan would work.

If not...

I'd be dead.

Chapter One — Four Months Later

DEANNA

Click, click, click. The sound of my fingers flying over the computer's keyboard was starting to annoy the fuck out of me. I turned up *Roachford* on my iPod sitting in its dock on my desk. My attention quickly went back to the monitor. *Buy, buy, and buy.* It was all I could think of.

Some thumps on my front door sounded over the music. I rolled my eyes because I already knew who it was. Groaning to myself, I put a halt on my online retail therapy and slid my chair back so I could bang my head against the desk. She was never going to get the fucking hint I wanted to be left alone for a while. I didn't want to taint her happiness with my... bitchiness.

"Open the flipping door, Deanna. I'm a woman on edge. I had a large slushy on the way over, *and* I'm six months pregnant. Do you want me to pee on your doorstep for all your neighbours to see?" Zara yelled.

Fuck it.

I shouldn't have turned up the music because now she knew I was definitely home, and *I* knew she wouldn't be ignored this time.

"Come on, cupcake; she's going to blow," Julian joined in on the yelling.

Scoffing, I got up and started for the front door of my two-story house. On the way, I took in the sight surrounding me. There was no way I could hide anything in the next two seconds, so I opened the door and prepared myself for hell.

"You." Zara glared as she cupped her hoo-ha with one hand while the other was pointing a finger at me. "We have some talking to do, wench, but move, 'cause I've gotta go." She pushed past me and ran for the bathroom that was down the hall off the lounge room, only her steps faltered before she reached the hall's doorway. "What the truck?" She gaped at everything around her.

"Incubator, we'll talk about how crazy our girl is after you pee," Julian said as he stepped through the front door and kissed me on my cheek.

I shut the front door and was geared up to knock myself out when Julian squealed behind me. I spun around and saw him clutching the *Ouran High School Host Club* DVD box set to his chest.

"Oh, my gawd! I-I've wanted this for years, but Mattie said if I got it he'd turn me out. Holy capoly, girlfriend, be prepared to have me living at your house so that I can watch this day-in and day-out." He sighed.

"Keep it," I said.

Julian eyed me suspiciously. He leisurely took me in from head to toe and then back again. "You look like shit."

I rolled my eyes and went back over to my desk, sat down and hit buy. A notice popped up on the screen announcing I was now the proud owner of a house in the Grampians.

Even though my eyes were still on the screen, I knew exactly when Zara had come back out. She stood behind me and slapped me on the back of the head.

"What the fuck?" I spun my computer chair around and glared up at her.

"What the duck, indeed," she hissed. "What is going on here, Deanna? I haven't seen you in two, nearly three months, and this is what I find when I finally catch you at home?" She gestured to the room around her. "Are you starting your own Target store? What is with all this crap?"

All this crap was the only thing I hoped would keep... *him* from coming after his—well, what he thought was his —inheritance. If I spent nearly every penny, he'd have no reason to hunt me down.

However, I couldn't tell Zara any of that. She was in a happy place after having been through her own hell. I wouldn't bring her down again.

I shrugged. "Just doin' a little shopping."

She turned to Julian, who was still fawning over his DVDs. "Do you believe her lies?"

"Hen pecker, I believe her lies are so big I could roll them in a joint and be high off them for a year."

"See? We don't believe you." She pulled me out of my chair and studied my face. "Hun, please, please tell me what this is all about. And I mean everything—why you've been avoiding us, and why your house looks like a… a hoarder's place."

"Do you guys want a coffee?" I asked instead of answering. Though, making a quick escape to the kitchen didn't work; they followed me.

"Don't make me bring in the big guns to get you talking, Deanna Drake."

I laughed. "What, your mum?" I walked around the

bench and readied the coffeemaker, and then turned to them as they sat at the kitchen counter.

"No—" she began.

I interrupted her. "Is that where Maya and Cody are?" I asked. Zara and Talon had won full custody for Cody two months ago, and they were ecstatic about it. So was Cody; he loved Zara, even more than his own mother. Though, no one could blame the kid; his mom was a slut.

"They're at school. Do you even know what day it is?"

"Sure, I was just fuckin' testing you, making sure you knew where your kids were. 'Cause you know, once your tribe pops out of you, you're gonna have to be on your toes."

"Bullshit." Julian coughed into his hand, then waved it in the air. "Basic manoeuvre to change the subject."

"That's the truth." Zara glared. "That's it. If you don't start talking, I'm calling." She grabbed her phone from her jeans pocket and opened it, fingers ready to dial.

"It's nothing you need to worry about, bitch."

"Five seconds, Deanna."

"Seriously?"

"Four seconds," she chimed.

"Who the fuck are you gonna call?" I snapped.

"The boss-man." She smiled.

"No," I gasped and shook my head.

"Yep. My hubby is already on speed dial. Four seconds, hun."

"Jesus, lamb chop, you're up to three seconds. Preggo brain strikes again," Julian said and sighed.

"If you call him, I will seriously be pissed at you," I informed her, and then leaned against the kitchen bench with my arms crossed over my chest.

"I'm willing to take your pissed-off mood if it gets me to the bottom of what's going on with you."

I closed my eyes and sighed. "Zara, *please* just leave it be."

"Oh, shit," Julian gasped. "She sounds serious, baby doll. S-she said please, and without cussing."

Zara nodded and said to me, "I know, but I can't let you deal with whatever you are on your own, Deanna. Friends don't do that. Also, if I recall correctly, it wasn't that long ago you were at my side through all my hell, and you wouldn't listen to me when I wanted it left well enough alone."

"Sing it, sister. Testify!" Julian yelled.

With a roll of my eyes, I said, "But look at how well all that turned out. And that was nearly a year ago."

"Tell me, Deanna," she pleaded.

I shook my head. "It's fine—nothing."

"Deanna!"

"Zara! Just let this blow over, and then everything will be back to normal." *I hope.*

"Let what blow over, buttercup?" Julian asked.

Shit!

"Nothin'. Look, I got crap to do, so both of you can just fuck off outta here."

Zara frowned, shook her head and then uttered, "One." She pressed her phone to her ear.

Fuck no!

I ran around the bench intending to tackle her for the phone, but she must have known that would have been my first move. She ran from the room.

"Hey, honey," I heard her say into the phone as I chased after her.

"Zara!" I yelled. "Don't you fuckin' dare." I glared as she stood on the other side of the couch.

"That's just Deanna in a bad mood."

"I will kill you," I hissed through clenched teeth.

"Why, you ask, is Deanna in a bad mood? Well, honey, I'm not sure, but there is something wrong here, Talon. I'm worried."

Motherfucker.

I knew I had no chance now. If Zara was worried, Talon would try his best to squish that worry for her—in any way he could.

I was done for.

Shit. No, I wasn't. I was Deanna Drake, and I didn't let anyone tell me what to do.

"Yeah," she said into the phone. "Thanks, honey. I'll see you soon." She flipped the phone closed, and put it in her pocket while biting her bottom lip.

Yeah, she should be worried. I was going to do what any tough, don't-fuck-with-me woman would do.

I ran from the room, up the stairs and locked myself in my bedroom.

My door shook as it got pounded on. “Open the fuckin' door, Hell Mouth,” Talon barked.

There was no way in hell I was opening my door. I was sure I could wait out the lot of them.

“Just leave.” I groaned from where I lay on my bed with my arm over my eyes.

“You know I won't. You're worrying my woman, Hell Mouth. I can't let that happen. Not only fuckin' that, but who her people are, now are Hawks’ people, and you're one of 'em. We help each other, and that means either come out here and tell me what in Christ’s name is goin' on, or *I* come in there.”

I snorted... and wiped away the stinking tears that broke free while I thanked fuck no one could see how his words had turned me into some stupid emotional woman.

But they had.

Because of Zara, I now had a family, one that was alive and willing to help. Jesus, I knew I had become a raging bitch when Zara wouldn't let anyone help with her problem, and now I was doing the same.

Ironic. Insert eye roll.

But this was different.

Now I understood why Zee was so damned determined to keep others safe from her crazy ex because right then, I was willing to do the same. The only difference was that the wanker who would soon be after me wasn't an ex.

Fucking hell.

Was I stupid with this act? Probably.

But I didn't want anyone to see the scared fucker I was becoming underneath this facade. I thought I could take on everything.

I was wrong.

I was weak.

And I hated it. I hated myself.

David, Zee's weirdo ex, helped prove how much of a wuss I was.

It was a week after Zee's episode with him that Talon called me in the middle of the night asking me if I wanted my payback, and if I did, I had to get my ass to Pyke's Creek.

What I thought I was prepared to do ended up being different than what I did do.

ACKNOWLEDGEMENTS

I would like to thank my sister, Rachel, for your help and how you've always believed in me. I would never have gotten this finished if it wasn't for you.

Nicole, for being my inspiration for the character Deanna, and for telling me to get my arse into gear to finish this. I love your guts, woman.

My family, Craig for giving me the time to complete this while you worked liked a mad man. Shayla and Jake for putting up with me through this all.

I would love to thank my critiquing friends, Nicola, Maggie and Pat. Without your help, I would have gone grammar crazy.

To my beta readers, Justine, Sue and Debbie. Your kind words helped me think that this wasn't in my imagination. I did have something to work with.

To Hot Tree Editing, Becky (you rock) and her crew, especially Kayla the Bibliophile and all my other wonderful editors. I want to thank you all for the great work you've done to make *Holding Out* better. Also for putting up with me and all my questions.

Lastly, I would like to thank Mum, Andrew, Tracey and Vicki for your encouragement.

ALSO BY LILA ROSE

Hawks MC: Ballarat Charter

Holding Out (FREE) Zara and Talon

Climbing Out: Griz and Deanna

Finding Out (novella) Killer and Ivy

Black Out: Blue and Clarinda

No Way Out: Stoke and Malinda

Coming Out (novella) Mattie and Julia

Hawks MC: Caroline Springs Charter

The Secret's Out: Pick, Billy and Josie

Hiding Out: Dodge and Willow

Down and Out: Dive and Mena

Living Without: Vicious and Nary

Walkout (novella) Dallas and Melissa

Hear Me Out: Beast and Knife

Breakout (novella) Handle and Della

Fallout: Fang and Poppy

Standalones related to the Hawks MC

Out of the Blue (Lan, Easton, and Parker's story)

Out Gamed (novella) (Nancy and Gamer's story)

Outplayed (novella) (Violet and Travis's story)

Romantic comedies

Making Changes

Making Sense

Fumbled Love

Trinity Love Series

Left to Chance

Love of Liberty (novella)

Paranormal

Death (with Justine Littleton)

In The Dark

CONNECT WITH THE AUTHOR

Webpage: www.lilarosebooks.com
Facebook: http://bit.ly/2du0taO
Instagram: www.instagram.com/lilarose78/
Goodreads:
www.goodreads.com/author/show/7236200.Lila_Rose